THE GOOD CHILDREN

Morag Higgins

Fisher King Publishing

THE GOOD CHILDREN

Copyright © Morag Higgins 2021

Print ISBN 978-1-914560-32-3
Digital ISBN 978-1-914560-33-0

This is a work of fiction. Names, characters, businesses, places, events and incidents are either the products of the author's imagination or used in a fictitious manner. Any resemblance to actual persons, living or dead, or actual events, is purely coincidental.

Published by
Fisher King Publishing
The Old Barn
York Road
Thirsk
YO7 3AD
England

www.fisherkingpublishing.co.uk

To Tess and Tag, your pawprints will
be in my heart forever and Skye,
your incessant yakking will always
ring in my ears. Will see you all
again over the rainbow bridge.

Also by or co-authored by
Morag Higgins

Bruja

Equido

Eye of the Unicorn

Equido - The Path of Least Resistance

CHAPTER ONE

They sat together, bewildered amongst the raucous jostling of their siblings. One slightly aloof and distant, the other anxious and insecure, but both seemingly drawn to each other, a silent bond of support holding them together. Their young infant minds strived to make sense of the world around them, a world of legs, sounds, smells and feelings, sensing that this was not really their place.

Their first mother gently pulled them to her warm soft body, squeezing them between everyone else as they all climbed over each other and snuggled close. Unable to form words, the brother and sister instinctively pushed closer together, their bond forged amongst the competitive world they had been born into.

Mama would quietly tell them all stories about her daily escapades when she would disappear and leave them alone to fend for themselves. Dada would occasionally come into the room and stare at them with mild curiosity, but no other desire to care for or to intervene in the disputes that would break out amongst them as hunger overcame play. When Mama returned, she made sure they were all clean and fed, doing her best to ensure a fair share was had by all, but with fourteen children, it was tricky. As they lay together keeping warm, Mama warily greeted Dada as he graced them with one of his visits.

Her look and stillness made it clear to him that he could be on his way; she wasn't interested in his bravado and boasting, not with this lot to care for.

In a short time, their strength grew and their legs were just that little bit longer, allowing them to explore their surroundings. It was a noisy affair with shouting and laughing in excitement at the prospect of adventures with Mama. They would try to follow her out of the house, their little legs clumsy and uncoordinated. The brother and sister would follow, sometimes in the middle of the crowd and sometimes bringing up the rear, the cautious nature of the boy and the aloofness of the girl causing them to think before they leapt. At night, Mama began to tell them about the outside world.

"You must all be brave and never be afraid," she would say, "People will come for you soon. You will have a new mother and father, and people are generally good." She would trail off in her story, a look of concern and worry in her eyes. She knew she could no longer care for her children; there were just too many and not enough food, so they must go.

"It will be exciting. You will have such adventures!" She tried to make it sound like a good thing, but it broke her heart to let them go. She had decided to keep two with her but could not decide who. The brother and sister would push just that bit closer to each other, seeming to understand more than the others that they would never see their mama again.

Then one day it happened. A new mama came. The girl was picked up and stared at a smiling face in front of her. She wasn't sure about this new mama; could she be trusted? A panic filled her; what about her brother? He couldn't cope without her. Then to her relief she saw her new mama pick up her brother and tuck him under her other arm. They both looked at each other as they were carried out into the big wide world; at least they would be together. They were taken to what seemed like a box with wheels, which they would later learn was a car. They were placed inside on a layer of soft blankets.

"There you go, sweeties, nice and warm." The new mama beamed happily at the two faces staring back at her. "I will call you Tess," she pointed to the girl, "and you are called Tag." The boy looked at her with worried eyes, hoping that he would be loved and cared for. The new mama looked back at Tess, "You look like a little princess with that haughty face. You must be Princess Tess, and you, well, you are definitely a Mr Tiggy McTaggle." She laughed and closed the door. The brother and sister looked at each other.

"New Mama says I'm a princess." The girl stared at the boy, who licked his lips and gazed worriedly around him.

"New Mama says I'm…" He paused, trying to

remember exactly what had been said, but there had been an awful lot of words for a young mind. "I'm Tiggy Tag." He nodded to himself, satisfied he'd done his best.

"Don't worry, Tag. I'll look after you." Tess licked his face just like their first mama had done to comfort them. Tag licked her back.

"Thank you, Princess Tess."

"You can call me Tess," she said as she straddled her four paws to balance better.

"And you can call me Tag." He stood a little taller and a lot braver with his sister beside him.

The shaking box stopped and the door opened, causing Tess and Tag to blink in the bright light. "Now then, wee babies, let's go and meet Uncle Jook." Their new mama picked them up, tucked them under each arm, and carried them into their new den. From their vantage point, Tess and Tag stared down at the big dog staring back at them with old eyes. Their noses coloured him with an array of scents, all unique to him.

"Well, Jooky boy, who's this then?" Their new mama put them down on the floor, more scents flooding into their brains. Old Jook regarded them, his nose slowly twitching from side to side as he took in their name smells. He lowered his head to the crouching figures in front of him, unsure and anxious at the large face peering at them. He grunted to himself.

"Well now, little ones, welcome to the pack. Stick

with me and I'll keep you right. Our leaders are strong and strict, so don't step out of line or you will be sorry." He gave them a stern look. "I'm Jook." He lay down in front of them and they regarded him cautiously, smelling he was kind and gentle.

"I'm Tag."

"And I'm a Princess." Tess gave him a haughty look, but Jook wasn't fooled for a moment.

"Are you now?"

"You can call me Tess." She puffed out her chest and tried to look important. Jook nudged her with his nose and she fell over.

"I'll decide what I call you. Until you can push me over with your nose, I'm in charge, got it?" His hard stare caused them both to quickly agree and he softened. Another two-leg came into the den.

"Is this them?" Mark looked down at the beautiful little puppies in front of Jook and grinned. "They're gorgeous." He picked them up and cuddled them.

"Lick his face, they love that," said Jook, watching as Tess and Tag enthusiastically licked the two-leg's face. "That is your new dad, but believe me, it's your mum that's in charge." Their new mama came back and took Tess from Mark.

"Who's a wee sweetie then?" Morag laughed as Tess tried to nibble her nose. "Ah no, no teeth!" She sat down and her faithful old Jook laid his head on her lap, looking at the new arrival. "You're still my best boy, Jooky, Mummy loves you very much." She kissed the old dog's head and he beamed with pride. "You've got your work cut out training these two," she said, and Jook agreed.

CHAPTER TWO

The first night alone away from the comfort of their siblings and First Mama was frightening. Tess and Tag huddled together in the warm blankets and listened to the sound of their new pack sleeping in another room. Jook was given the honoured position of sleeping next to the pack leaders and they knew they would have to earn that right by being good. They had each other. Tag rhythmically licked Tess, and every so often she would return the gesture till finally they both fell asleep, dreaming of warm milk and their first mama's touch.

The grey light of dawn filtered into the den through the curtains as Tess and Tag slowly started to wake up. Tag whined anxiously.

"I need to go pee and poo," he said, staring at the wire cage in front of their bed. Their first mama had taught them well; never make a mess in your bed, do it outside. For them, outside had been on paper laid down next to their sleeping box, but now they couldn't get out to go.

"I need to pee and poo too." Tess pawed the cage and started to whimper and yowl. Sounds of stirring filtered through to them from the other room and New Mama came through, old Jook at her heels.

"Hey there, sweeties, need the toilet?" She opened the den door first then made her way back to the bed cage.

Jook glanced over his shoulder as he went outside.

"Don't embarrass me, do your business outside the den."

Tag was really bursting. Two-leg Dad came through and picked him up as New Mama took Tess. They were whisked out of the cage and very quickly taken outside to the green grass just in time. They both peed in relief.

"Good boys and good girlie!" the leaders said enthusiastically. Tess and Tag could smell they were happy with them and grinned up, their little tails wagging. Jook wagged his tail at them as well.

"Well now, you held on just long enough." He nodded with approval as they both sat down and had a poo. "Remember that this never happens in the den."

"Our first mama taught us that!" said Tess indignantly. "We didn't mess our beds."

"Not messing your beds is one thing," said Jook, "Not messing in the larger den is another." Tess and Tag looked at each other; it was true. If they had not been carried out quickly by the leaders, they would have messed in the big den.

"We promise to try to hold on," said Tag as he pottered over to Jook on stubby baby legs.

"Good lad," said Jook and he offered a play-bow. "Want to play chase?"

"Yaaay!" Tess and Tag shouted. Uncle Jook was fun.

Those first few months were crammed with things to learn. At first, Tess and Tag would be full of energy and play for a short while, Mama and Dad spending time playing with them and teaching them the rules. Then suddenly they would be exhausted, falling asleep almost on the spot. Sometimes they managed to crawl into their beds themselves, closing their eyes as the cage door clicked shut, giving their humans two hours of peace and time for them to catch up on their work. Then it was wide awake time for both of them, yapping to be released, keen and full of energy.

As they grew larger and the time spent awake grew longer, Mama made a playpen outside for them full of toys and tunnels and things to climb on; it was great. She would put them in the pen and they laughed and ran, biting at each other and playing chase. Uncle Jook would sometimes watch them, but his job was to patrol the yard and keep a nose out for intruders. At night, he would lie and talk to them about being dogs, what the dog rules were and how to behave. Tess and Tag would curl up beside him as he told them stories of his adventures running along behind the horses, and he explained how to behave around these large and potentially dangerous animals.

Eventually, the children (as Mama called them) were too big for the pen; they were able to climb out over the low wall and run after Mama and Dad. This was where Jook took his responsibilities very seriously. He would chaperone them, keeping them out of trouble and teaching them all the smell names their tiny noses were now exposed to. Dogs don't see a lot of colour with their eyes, but with smell, well – to a dog, a scent is like a bright colour, each one having its own shade and hue depending on how old it is (the older it is, the more pastel it appears). New scents are brilliantly strong, so although dogs don't see colours as humans do, their world is far more vibrant, with everything wrapped in its own scent rainbow.

Jook patiently taught the children about grass and all the smell colours it came in, and about the other animals that shared their world and would pass through, leaving ghost-like images of themselves as scents. There was just so much to learn, but their young minds were keen and eager, and learn they did. The best time was when each one spent their own special time with Mama as she taught them the human rules (Jook had explained about humans). She would gently and patiently teach them to sit, stay, lie down, and come back to her. The best thing was they got a special treat if they got it right. Tag was so eager to please that he would get himself in a tizzy trying to do the right thing. Mama would just laugh and ask him to be calm, which he found very hard to do.

The best teacher was Jook, and Mama would enlist his help if she wanted them to come back. She would shout to Jook first and he would respond immediately. This encouraged Tess and Tag to respond too, as they knew there would be a treat in store. Tess was always more wilful and independent, so Mama had to be very sure she obeyed before getting the treat. Tag learned faster. Dad thought Tess was a bit stupid, but she was just a princess and no one bossed a princess. She knew better than to be disobedient as Jook would step in with a disapproving look or comment. Eventually, she deigned to comply and became as obedient as Tag.

The summer was long and hot, and the children grew strong and fast. Jook was beginning to slow down a bit and would spend most of his time just watching through hazy eyes, his nose telling him more about what was going on. Tess and Tag would play chase for hours on end, running into one stable (only when the horses were out) under the partition and out the other stable door. They would run in circles like this for ages, taking turns to chase or be chased. Once that game was over, they would play explorers and sniff about the horse yard, guessing what animals had passed there during the night.

One day, two people and another dog turned up in the yard. Jook ran excitedly around the car, shouting, "Jess, Jess, it's me, how are you?" A tall, slim, elderly hound jumped out of the boot and enthusiastically licked Jook in the face.

"Jook, my dearest friend, I'm so pleased to see you

again! It seems like ages since we last met." She regarded the two young puppies running about the new humans, yapping and shouting for attention. "Is this them? The new puppies I've heard my mum and dad talk about?"

"Yes, it is. They're learning." Jook wagged his tail and went to greet Old Mum and Dad. Morag's parents bent down to pat the old dog's head as Jess regarded the puppies.

"So, what are your names?" Jess looked down her nose at them. Tess had thought she was a princess, but here, well, here was a dog that had all the elegance and majesty you could ever imagine.

"I'm Tag!" shouted Tag with gusto and bounded towards Jess to greet her. He was stopped short by a warning growl.

"I don't do noisy greetings and you will not jump about me, do you hear?"

"Yes, I'm sorry." Tag hung his head and cowered, showing his belly to Jess, who sniffed him thoroughly.

"And you are?" She looked at Tess.

"I'm Princess Tess," was the reply as Tess cautiously, almost defiantly, walked over to Jess. As she got closer, her bravado broke and she cowed down submissively like Tag. Jess gave her a cursory sniff.

"I like your attitude, but remember, I'm in charge." She turned and bounded into the large den (which the children now understood was a caravan) without even using the steps. Jook slowly walked up behind her and into the den, leaving Tess and Tag to stare at each other.

"But this is our territory!" Tess was annoyed and confused.

"Jook knows her well so she must be treated the same as him," said Tag. They bounded up the steps and into the den to see what was going on.

Aunty Jess came to visit at least once a week, but for a dog, a week was more like a month. So although they got to know her, it was the stories that Jook told them about their adventures together that made her part of the pack. Tess and Tag realised very quickly that they were part of a very large and very strong pack mostly made up of human aunties and uncles, some of which they would only meet every few months, but others were in their lives for a long, long time. It made them feel secure and safe knowing there were so many people looking out for them and loving them, but Tess felt especially close to Uncle Jook. Tag was bigger and stronger than Tess with longer legs; he specialised in speed.

On one rare occasion when Aunty Jess was visiting, she watched Tag running up and down the long grass stretch in front of the stables. He was chasing crows.

"What are you trying to do?" she asked him.

"I'm the guard of this pack, it's my job to keep intruders away, and crows are the worst," he said proudly.

"You're not fast enough to catch a crow," she said indulgently.

"Am so!" Tag lifted his puppy nose, which was now almost level with Jess's chin. She looked at him and grinned a doggie grin.

"Are you as fast as this?" She turned and ran. Jess was an old dog, about twelve years, but she was a lurcher and speed had always been her strength. Despite her years, she felt for a moment the flush of youth as she opened up her long stride, the lithe muscular body powering her along the grass patch. She wasn't nearly as fast as she had been in her younger days, but she left Tess and Tag standing.

"Wow!" said Tag, suitably impressed as he raced as fast as he could to keep up.

Tess ran behind them shouting, "Wait for me! Wait for me!", her bark echoing around the yard. Jess stopped at the end of the yard and waited till they had caught up.

"Now, young Tag, when you can run like that then maybe you will catch a crow." She was panting heavily, not used to such exertion. She started to jog back to Jook, who had been watching the excitement from his comfortable seat in the grass.

"I'll practise…" Tag was puffing between strides. "I'll be as fast one day, wait and see."

"I'm fast too," protested Tess, frustrated that her legs were so much shorter than Tag's. She stopped in front of

Jook, who nodded to her to come closer.

"Sometimes, Tess, speed isn't everything. You have to use your brain and your nose too." He grinned and she grinned back. She loved Uncle Jook.

Aunty Jess (as she became known) would visit regularly with Old Mum and Dad, and it was on one of these visits that Jess began to act oddly. She jumped down from the car and bounded up the steps into the caravan as normal, but her face was drawn and her lips tight. Uncle Jook looked at her in a strange way, his nose twitching from side to side. Tag and Tess wagged their tails and welcomed Aunty Jess, but she smelt strange. They couldn't quite put their noses on it. She had the same name smell, but underneath, there was something else – something bitter, something strange. Tess wrinkled her nose and stared at Jess whilst Tag gently play-bowed in front of her.

"Come and run outside, Jess. I'm almost as fast as you now!" Jess didn't answer and turned her head away, lying down with a distant look in her eyes. Tag stood bemused and Tess was unsure.

"Come away and leave her alone," said Jook, "She is tired." The young puppies didn't understand. They could sense the worry in Jook, but they were obedient children and did as they were told, lying together, quietly watching Jess as her name smell grew fainter.

Another human week passed and Jess had not come

to visit, nor had Old Mum and Dad. Everyone was in the main room of the caravan when the phone call came.

"Mark." Morag was really upset. "Can you go over to Mum and Dad's quickly? She needs help to get Jess to the vet. She's collapsed." The dogs could see the smell colours of fear, sadness, and something else, something the youngsters had never seen before. It was a muddy grey colour and it drowned out everything else. There was a bitter tang to the smell as well and it upset Tess and Tag. Jook just lay quietly and watched his Mum, waiting for her to sit down as Dad drove away. He stood up and sat beside her, leaning on her leg, his heart full of comfort and love.

"That, young pups, is the scent of grief."

"What is grief?" they asked.

"It is a pain that you feel, an emptiness left by someone you love not being here anymore. I think Jess will not be coming back." He fell silent. The puppies smelled the colour of grief washing over him too.

It was two human weeks later when Old Mum and Dad came again. There was no Aunty Jess jumping out of the car, just a box with a strange scent to it. Jook twitched his nose and welcomed the humans, eyeing the box in sadness.

"Uncle Jook, what is that scent?" asked Tess. She was really working hard at developing her nose.

"What does it smell like?" asked Jook patiently. Tess thought for a moment.

"It smells of cold fire and… Aunty Jess?" She looked at Jook in confusion. Jook just nodded sadly and turned away.

"You have a good nose, Tess, a very good nose."

The whole pack walked into a small grove in the woodland next to the yard where Dad had dug a hole. The humans were all crying and Jook sniffed around the glade, pretending not to notice what was going on. Tag and Tess jumped and ran in excitement, trying to cheer up the humans, but eventually, even they became quiet as the box was put into the hole and covered up.

"Jess will always be here now," said Jook.

"What did they put in the hole, Uncle Jook?" asked Tag as they all walked back to the caravan. Jook just looked at him sadly.

"Something very precious, Tag. Jess was my friend and now she is gone."

"Gone?" asked Tess, peering into the old dog's eyes.

"Her body was old and she couldn't use it anymore, so she left it behind."

"Where is she now?" asked Tag, sitting down and scratching his ear as he tried to understand. Jook sighed.

"That, my boy, is a big mystery. All I know is that sometimes we will see Jess as she comes to visit. Like an old scent that is almost gone, we will see her faintly.

We will know she is there. The humans buried Jess's body, or at least the ashes of her body. She doesn't need it anymore."

"What was that bitter smell that Aunty Jess had the last time she visited?" Tess was curious.

"That, my pups, is the scent of death." Jook turned and walked into the caravan never to talk about Jess again.

CHAPTER THREE

The summer faded and autumn came in a glory of colour, the crisp air sharp and a new array of scents filling Tag and Tess's noses. Jook as ever was indulgent and continued with his tutoring of his young students, but this cold weather no longer suited his old bones and joints, and he was beginning to struggle. The puppies ran and played on the hard frosty grass, loving the tickling sensation on their warm noses as the ice crystals from the blades melted away. They were growing up fast.

Mum and Dad were teaching them how to sit, stay and come on command, and each one tried to outdo the other at who was the best puppy. There was always a reward and love, even if they got it wrong. Tag would press his head against Mum's thigh and close his eyes in joy as he felt her hand gently caress his ear, love in every movement. Tess, ever the bold one, would push her nose (she just wasn't as tall as Tag) into Mum's hand as she walked along, and it became their special thing of Mum holding onto Tess's muzzle as they walked.

When the really wet and cold weather came, it was even more fun – puddles! These were just the best thing and so much fun. Tag and Tess would spend hours running and splashing through the muddiest deepest puddles they could find till any white markings they had were covered in a slick chocolatey mud pack.

"Uncle Jook, come and play in the mud!" they would shout together, but Jook just shook his head and sat in the hayshed out of the chill wind, taking pride in his pristine white legs.

"Look at the state of you pair!" Dad would exclaim, "Right, hose, now!" He would grab them by the collars and use the spray on the hose to get the worst of the mud off. They didn't mind; their coats were so thick that they didn't even feel the cold.

"Just wait till it gets really wintry," Jook would say as he watched them getting washed, "You won't want hosing then." He slowly made his way into the caravan.

One evening as they were all heading back in for dinner, Tess caught a scent on the breeze. She looked round but Tag and Jook were already in the caravan. Pausing, she waited till Mum caught up with her. The scent grew stronger in the twilight and Tess squinted her eyes as she saw something strange standing at the entrance to the outdoor arena. Lowering her head, she growled softly in her throat, unsure of what the strange shape was. There was something familiar about the scent too; it smelled like… Aunty Jess? Tess couldn't understand what she was seeing. Her nose told her it was Jess, but it wasn't a solid body in front of her. Instead, it was faint, transparent, like an old scent colour almost faded.

Mum caught up with her and followed her eye-line. Tess hoped she could see the dog in front of her that was slowly wagging its tail, a strange doggy grin on its face. Mum paused, holding her breath as she sensed what Tess was seeing. Tess stopped growling; it was definitely Aunty Jess, but younger. She whined, unsure of what to do. It was all very strange. Jess bowed in a play stance and grinned at her. Tess looked up at Mum but she wasn't looking at Jess, just at the gate to the school. Looking back, she wagged her tail at Aunty Jess, who was now rolling about on the grass.

Morag looked down at Tess, who was staring at the gate. Although she couldn't see what Tess saw, she had a pretty good idea of what it was.

"It's alright, baby, it's only Aunty Jess come to visit." She put her hand on Tess's head and felt her lean onto her thigh.

"Aunty Jess, where have you been?" Tess asked. Jess didn't answer. She moved her mouth as though she had barked, but no sound came. Instead, she faded till she had vanished, but her scent lingered for a few moments more. Mum turned and walked into the caravan with Tess following slowly behind, glancing over her shoulder, unsure about what had just happened. Mum was acting like it was OK, so shaking her head, she put it out of her mind and focused on the delicious dinner that was waiting for her.

The first winter for Tag and Tess was a wet and miserable one, but they didn't mind. They were with their pack and included in everything the humans did. They got up at 5.30 am with Mum and Dad, following them out onto the yard in bleak weather to 'help' do the horses. Uncle Jook would follow on, sitting in the hayshed and keeping out of the worst of the weather. He would shout encouragement to the youngsters as they trotted along behind the horses, making sure everyone got to the fields safely (of course, Mum and Dad were leading the horses, but it was up to Tag in particular to make sure everything was done correctly).

Once the horses were out, Uncle Jook would go back to the caravan for a snooze while Tag would start his yard patrol. He would wander up and down, checking in all the stables and making sure Mum and Dad were safe. Tess would practise sniffing out smells and putting together a picture of what animals had moved through the yard the previous night. Once all the stables had been mucked out (the babies never could understand why Mum and Dad threw away all the yummy-tasting horse droppings), it would be time for breakfast (although Tag and Tess would have been snacking on bits of horse dung Mum and Dad had missed).

Uncle Jook had educated the puppies well. They knew they must never, ever go into an arena while horses were in there, but when it was empty, well, it was just one big playpen. Tag would run full pelt around the open space shouting encouragement to Tess, who tried very hard to keep up. Tag was a speed specialist; he had never forgotten Aunty Jess and how fast she had run. He was determined to be the fastest dog in the world! Anytime Mum and Dad were not working horses or doing yard duties, they would play with the children, throwing toys and balls for them to chase.

Just before spring, there was a late flurry of snow as winter gave one last blast. Snow! It was amazing. Tag would run with his nose digging a furrow, revelling in the soft crunch of the cold, white, fluffy stuff that smelled like water. He would leap and pounce, snapping at the blanket of snow, Tess and Jook laughing at his antics. Tag loved to hear everyone laugh. He was such a kind, sensitive soul, wanting to make everyone happy. The best game was when Mum and Dad made snowballs and threw them across the yard. They would race each other to get the magic snowball first. It was always Tag that got there, but as he grabbed the ball, it would crumble in his mouth and vanish. He never could figure out where it went to.

When the snow had melted, it was back to mud. The caravan was struggling to cope with twelve muddy paws, so Mum set up a tray of water just outside the door, which she called the puppy bath. The puppies looked at the tray with suspicion, so it was Jook that led the way. His feet were always clean, but he understood that Mum wanted the youngsters to wash their feet before they went in, so he calmly stepped into the tray of water without being prompted by Mum and walked through it, cleaning his already white paws.

"See, it's perfectly safe," he said, grinning and slowly walking up the steps.

"You go first," said Tess, unsure. Tag cautiously put a paw in the cold water and looked up at Mum.

"It's OK, baby, just a wee adventure in the puppy bath."

Tag took a deep breath. He so wanted to make Mum happy and proud, so despite his worry, he walked into the tray and washed his feet.

"You're such a good boy, mummy's boy!" Morag cuddled him and kissed him on the head.

"Me next! I'm a good girl!" Tess didn't want to be left out so she splashed into the tray, washing her extremely dirty legs. The tray didn't get the mud above her paws, but Mum would give her a rub down with a towel in the caravan.

"Where's my little princess? You're a good wee girlie." Morag praised Tess and kissed her on the nose. Tess beamed with pride, and that was them set. Every day during the winter before they went into the caravan, Mum would shout "Into the puppy bath!" and they would all walk through the tray.

Tag loved his sister; she was his best friend. When

she was wet, he would lick her dry, comforting her as their first mama had done. Sometimes she would lick him back, but mostly they loved to just snuggle up together, content in their home with their pack. The caravan was cold in the winter, but Mum and Dad had put a soft warm bed in between the benches for the table (they had already taken the table away to accommodate the training cage). It was warm enough in this den curled up together through the night.

Uncle Jook had the privileged position next to Mum and Dad's bed, but as the winter progressed, he was finding it too uncomfortable to squeeze into the tight space between the wall and the bed, so he was given his own plastic bed in the main room next to the babies. He loved it there. He was finding that he was getting too hot and sometimes found it hard to breathe. The cold air in the living room was ideal and he would lie in his bed and tell stories to the puppies about his adventures with his horse friend Bruja. He loved to reminisce and sometimes he carried on talking after the puppies were fast asleep, occasionally catching a familiar scent as he would chat with his dearest friend Jess.

Spring came early and Tess and Tag were getting taller. Tag towered over Jook, his long legs and agile body giving him the speed he so desperately wanted. Tess was more like her uncle, shorter than Tag but powerfully built. She was nearly as fast as her brother but never seemed to quite catch him. Sometimes when they were playing fetch with Mum or Dad, Tag would deliberately slow down just to let Tess get close to him, then he would sprint and get the ball before her. She would run alongside him, barking madly, demanding he give her the ball. Occasionally he relented and dropped it for her to bring back to Mum and Dad.

Tess was lying next to Uncle Jook in the warm spring air. His eyesight was getting bad, cataracts clouding his vision, but his nose was as keen as always. Tag was patrolling, keeping a watch for his arch enemies, the crows.

"Why does he chase the crows?" asked Jook as he sniffed in Tag's direction. He had caught the scent of a raven on the wind and it was coming closer.

"It's like a game they play," replied Tess, "The crows call him names and try to get him to chase them, then they wait till the very last moment and fly away laughing."

Jook licked his lips; he was getting more and more thirsty these days. "He'll never catch them, you know."

"I know, but he loves to try." Tess heard a chirruping sound that she had never heard before. "What's that, Uncle Jook?"

Jook listened carefully; his hearing wasn't as good as it used to be, but his nose gave him the answer. "The swallows are back!" he said excitedly, "Summer is almost here!"

"What are swallows?" Tess was intrigued as her nose picked up the bright dazzling scent carried on the wind.

"Far travellers," said Jook, "They tell the strangest stories about the things they have seen. You should listen to them someday." Tess snorted.

"Listen to birds! They have no brains."

"They're smarter than Tag," said Jook and they both laughed.

Tag was poised, body tense; his prey had just landed. The big black bird eyed him and strolled casually around the grass, pecking at nothing in particular.

"Hey, fat boy!" the bird shouted, "You want a piece of me?" Tag curled his lip, lowering his body as he made ready for the sprint. If he let that stupid bird get a bit closer… The raven stared at Tag. "You deaf as well as stupid?" it said, cawing in raucous laughter. Tag edged closer, one slow step at a time. "Stupid doggy can't run for toffee," sang the raven as it hopped nearer, daring Tag to run.

In a burst of speed from his powerful back legs, Tag leapt forwards. He was flat out in a millisecond, taking the raven completely by surprise. Flapping its wings in shock, the bird fell back as it tried to lift itself into the air. Tag was almost on his target and realised that he was going to catch the bird, but that wasn't the game – the game was chase, so he slowed down a fraction to let the raven get into the air.

"Clear off, you sorry bunch of feathers!" he barked, knowing the bird knew he had let him go.

"Well, well, doggy, you won. I won't forget what you did." The raven landed on the fence post and bobbed up and down with a thankful bow. "I'll never come back, I promise."

"But you must come back," said Tag desperately, "I want to chase you again!" The raven looked at him, first with one eye then the other. It clacked its beak together deep in thought.

"OK, doggy, here's the deal; me and my friends will visit every so often, just to keep you on your toes, but only if you promise never to catch us."

"I promise," said Tag, grinning from ear to ear.

"It's a deal, fat…" The raven paused. "It's a deal, fast boy." With that, he jumped into the air and flew away. "Fast doggy nearly caught me!" His raucous chant carried away on the wind.

Tess and Tag were playing chase around the stables one morning and had paused for breath in one of the empty boxes. A fleeting flash of speeding feathers caught their attention as a small bird whizzed past and landed on the rafters, staring down at them. The name scent was exotic, telling of hot places and high winds. Tess remembered what Uncle Jook had called such a name scent.

"It's a swallow," she said, "Uncle Jook says that

means summer will be here soon."

"Well, fur hunters, you are new." The bird peered at them.

"Are not! Been here almost all of our lives," exclaimed Tag, "It's you that's new."

"Been here all of your lives?" the bird mocked Tag, "This is my nest site, always has been, so you'd better keep clear, got it?" The puppies blinked in surprise at such a small creature making such big demands. Tag's fur stood on end; this bird was instantly on the banned list.

"Listen, small feathers. I decide who stays and who is welcome, you got that?" He stared hard at the bird in the rafters. Tess curled her lip.

"You'd better do as he says, or I will get you." She showed her front teeth in a threat.

"Really? Well try and get me." The bird swooped down and circled their heads, clicking its beak at them, then was out the door before they could even react.

"I don't think I like swallows," said Tag under his breath.

They both strolled out and looked for Mum and Dad, hoping for a game of chase the ball. There was an angry chattering coming from the far end of the yard and the caw of a crow in annoyance. Tess and Tag watched with fascination as the tiny swallow dived and swooped at the crow, intimidating the bigger bird till it hopped away and jumped into the air. It landed on the outdoor school fence and looked at the two dogs.

"You fast, doggy?" The crow stared at Tag, who puffed out his chest with pride and nodded. "Well, see if your fast legs can help you catch annoying feathers over there." The crow looked round at the swallow, which was circling and singing above its chosen nesting stable.

"They are really rude," said Tess.

"Yep," replied the crow, "but their chicks taste good." Tess and Tag weren't sure what the crow meant but nodded anyway. "Want to chase me, doggy?" asked the crow. Tag lowered himself into a crouch, a low growl in his throat, then launched himself at the fence barking madly. "Not bad, fast boy, see you again." They watched as the crow flew away, singing to itself.

One warm day at the start of summer, Mum opened up the car boot and called Tess and Tag over. She picked them up and put them in the car. They were very excited – this was an adventure! They had seldom been in the car since they had arrived as little babies, so every journey promised to be great fun. Mum drove a short distance to another house where they could hear other dogs barking excitedly. Mum put on their leads and they jumped out of the car, following her into the garden where lots of exciting sights, sounds and smells bombarded them. There was a whole group of dogs shouting out "Me, my turn! Me, let me go!" all at the same time. Even though they didn't know why, Tess and Tag felt they had to join in. Mum shushed them into silence and chatted to another lady.

A smaller brown and white dog that looked a little like Jook was straining at his leash, fixated on a series of obstacles in the large garden.

"Hi, I'm Tag."

"And I'm Tess!" they said, trying to get the other dogs' attention.

"What? Oh, yes, hi, I'm Digger." The new dog barely noticed them; he was more interested in what was going on at the obstacles.

Tess looked at Tag, who shrugged. They looked round at two young black and white dogs, both staring with manic eyes at the proceedings.

"I am Tess. What's your name?" Tess pushed her nose politely towards the nearest black and white dog, a nose she nearly lost as the dog snapped at her, snarling.

"Get away from me! I don't speak to mongrels like you!"

"Leave her alone!" Tag leapt to Tess's defence as Mum pulled them both away.

Tess was shocked; she had never been snapped at before, and she was now a little nervous of all the other dogs around her. She backed away and accidentally bumped into yet another dog.

"I'm sorry, please don't bite me!" she exclaimed as she spun around to see who she had walked into. A happy smiling doggy face met hers.

"It's alright, kid, don't worry about the Collie. She's actually really nervous." The dog wagged his tail softly. "This your first time at agility?"

"What's agility?" asked Tag as he wagged his tail at the friendly dog.

"Well now," the friendly dog laughed, "It's about the best thing in the world besides a belly rub." Tess and Tag were intrigued; they didn't think there was anything better than a belly rub.

"Wow! That sounds great. What's your name?" asked Tess, her confidence returned.

"I'm Hoy, you know, Hoy the Boy."

"I'm Tag."

"I'm Tess."

"Well hello, Tag and Tess, nice to meet you. I think you guys are going to love doing agility." Hoy started to jump about with excitement. "Speak to you later. It's my turn!" His human let him off his lead and he ran excitedly towards what looked like small jumps (the puppies were already used to seeing the larger jumps the horses were ridden over). They watched in amazement as Hoy ran around a course of fences, leaping high over them all and having such a good time.

"This looks great fun!" Tag fidgeted on the lead, desperate to have a go.

"Me, me, me please!" Tess was almost turning herself

inside out.

Mama gave her lead to one of the other humans as she let Tag go first. Tess yowled in annoyance and frustration. The jumps were put down so that the poles were just on the ground, and so began Tag's first agility session. He was hooked. Once Tag had had a go, it was Tess's turn. By this time, she was so excited all she could do was bark and shout "Hurry up, Mum, where next?" as she ran about the course. By the end of the session, they were both addicted to this amazing new game. They sat in the back of the car, exhausted and elated, desperate to tell Uncle Jook about their adventures.

CHAPTER FOUR

Every week throughout the summer, Mum would take Tag and Tess to agility training. One week it would be Tag's turn, the next it would be Tess's turn. It was frustrating for whoever was left behind, but Uncle Jook did his best to cheer them up by asking them to tell him all about what they had learned. They grew to love the car as it meant they were going on an adventure! To get extra practice in between training sessions, Mum had brought home a couple of the small jumps and things called weave poles. This was one of the hardest tasks the puppies had ever been asked to do and they needed all the practice they could get.

It was a hot summer's day. Uncle Jook had been very tired and quiet all week, but today he was like a young dog again. He even ran with the puppies as they bounded down the drive to greet some clients who had just arrived. Mama had set up the weave poles and Jook sat watching how she tempted Tess and Tag in turn to weave their bodies through the poles with a piece of chicken held in her hand. If they did it right, they got the chicken. When the session was nearly over, Jook got up and stood at the poles. Morag looked at the game old dog.

"You want to try, Jooky boy?" Jook grinned his old doggy grin and Mama put a piece of chicken under his nose, slowly guiding him through the weave poles.

"Way to go, old man, that was brilliant!" She gave him the rest of the chicken. Jook had never felt prouder. He turned to Tess and Tag, who were wagging their tails in encouragement.

"Looks like you can teach an old dog new tricks!" he laughed wheezily.

Tess caught the scent of something on his breath. Her tail stopped wagging as her nose twitched, trying to identify the strange smell. She stared at Jook, who looked at her kindly.

"It's OK, Tess. I know." Tess whined and gently licked his face.

Mama went back to the horses and they all followed. Jook lay down in his usual spot on the grass in front of the feed room; it was cool there and he could catch the scents from all directions. No horses were allowed on this grass so he was safe from being stood on. He lay down in the warm sun and dozed off.

It was late in the day and Dad shouted the puppies in for their dinner. As Tess ran past Jook, who was sound asleep, she barked at him to hurry up or he would miss his supper.Jook woke up and paused for a moment. He felt strange; something was wrong. He stood up on his old legs but they didn't want to support his weight, so he lay down again. And waited.

Mama was watching him from the feed room. "Hey, old man, you OK?" He looked at her and she looked at him, knowing that it was not OK. Morag turned to the client standing next to her. "I think it's time. I'll call the vet tomorrow."

"He'll be fine," said the client, knowing he wouldn't be.

Morag walked over to her faithful old friend and gently touched his head. "Come on, old man, let's go in." Jook gathered himself together and stood up stiffly. He just felt so tired. His legs wouldn't move fast, but Mum walked very slowly beside him so that he would be where he always had been – by her side.

He mustered the last of his strength and made his way up the steps into the caravan, stepping into his basket and lying down, utterly exhausted. Tess and Tag looked up at Mum and Dad, who were staring at each other, the scent of sadness floating down. Tag looked at Tess.

"What's wrong with Uncle Jook?" he asked, a small whine in his throat.

"I don't know," said Tess, "He smells like… like Aunty Jess did the last time she visited." They both looked at their mentor, who was now fast asleep in his bed.

"Here we go, children." Mum put their food down in front of them, leaving Jook's on the kitchen worktop. The puppies ate their meals but their appetite was gone. Once finished, they both lay down in their beds and watched Uncle Jook sleep.

All that evening, Mama sat beside Jook, her hand resting on his shoulder as he slept. Jook always felt safe when he was touching his Mum or Dad, and feeling her hand there made him feel better. He was tired, exhausted. As the night grew dark, he dreamed of Jess laughing and running about him, and there in the green fields was Bruja, his horse friend – she was running and bucking, daring him to come and chase her. His breathing grew fainter, more laboured. He could still feel Mum's hand, but the green field was so bright and the scents so intriguing. Bruja galloped past with Jess in hot pursuit. Jook felt Mum's hands take his head, his breathing shallow and faint.

"It's OK, old man, it's OK. Where's Bruja? Go get Bruja, go get her." He could see Mum's eyes; they were full of tears and her scent was grief, but she had said it was OK and he trusted her. He could hear Jess call him and Bruja laugh. The grass scent was strong again – he was strong again. The caravan melted away and he was there standing in the green, green field, his body strong as he sprinted after his friends.

Tess and Tag lay very still as they watched Mum and Dad crying beside Uncle Jook. The scent was clear now; his name scent was fading and almost gone, and now the bitter scent of death was growing stronger. A car pulled up outside the caravan and Old Mum and Dad made their way into the living room, pausing to stroke Jook's head as he lay still with his eyes closed, curled up in his basket. The humans all sat and talked, drinking tea and crying, looking at Jook. Tess and Tag had come out to greet Old Mum and Dad as they came in, then they had both sniffed Jook, Mum cuddling them and telling them it was alright.

Eventually, Old Mum and Dad left and the lights went out as Mum and Dad went to bed. Tag felt so sad and lost, and Tess was really upset. She went over to Jook and stared at him, her nose taking in the fading scent name, perplexed as the death scent was no longer bitter but calming and quiet. She curled up beside her uncle and Tag joined her. They knew no other way to express their grief; they couldn't cry like the humans, so instead, they wept inside.

In the morning, Mum and Dad found them still lying beside Jook and patted them all, gently stroking Jook's cold head. Dad went out early, taking Tess and Tag with him. They went into the woodland next to the grazing field. Normally, the puppies loved this treat – they would run ahead, galloping through the trees, chasing insects and taking in the myriad of different scents and sounds – but today was different. They trotted ahead of Dad understanding they were going to do something important. They went to the place where they had buried the box smelling of Jess. A short distance away from the stone marking the spot, Dad started to dig another hole. Tag wanted to help him dig, but he knew it would be wrong as it wasn't a game. Instead, he and Tess wandered around the small grove keeping a watchful eye on Dad's progress.

Eventually, he called their names and they all made their way back to the caravan.There to greet them was Old Mum and Dad; they watched as Jook was wrapped in his blanket and carried to the hole in the woods. Everyone was so sad. Tag did his best to gently reassure them all, putting his head against their thighs, Tess sticking her nose into their hands, looking for comfort. Old Jook was buried beside his friend, a stone marking his spot and his plastic bed upside-down over the grave to protect it. Tess and Tag knew they wouldn't see him again, but over the years, Tess would sometimes catch his scent – faint, carried on the wind like a whisper, but it was there. When she sensed it, she would smile to herself.

Summer that year was hot and glorious. The swallows had arrived in force with several pairs selecting their nest sites in the stables. Word seemed to have gotten around the bird community about Tag loving to chase anything that flew, and the swallows were keen to get in on the act. They worked in teams to torment poor Tag, swooping past his head and clicking their beaks at him. "Slow doggie can't catch us!" they would shout, which infuriated Tag no end. He would race up the grass in front of the stables flat out with a swallow deliberately flying just in front of his nose, teasing him as he could almost grab its tail feathers. As he ran out of grass, it would fly up and another would take its place, goading Tag into chasing it back along the yard. The swallows thought this was hysterically funny and Tag would be barking in frustration as he ran flat out, getting hotter and more exhausted as the naughty swallows just wouldn't let up. Eventually, Mum would intervene and put Tag into the caravan to rest and cool down. He would glare over his shoulder at the laughing birds as he was marched inside – he didn't think he liked swallows much.

Tess just couldn't figure out what the attraction was. She knew she didn't have any chance of catching a swallow as it flew past, so she would wait, pretend not to notice, sniffing around the stable doors and biding her time. One day, a swallow made the mistake of getting too close and SNAP! Tess grabbed it by the tail feathers before it could get away, pulling it out of the air. "AHHHH," screeched the little bird as it fell to the ground. Tess was as amazed as the swallow as she stared at it, the plucked feathers still in her mouth. The swallow didn't hang around; it leapt into the air and flew a little unsteadily up to the roof of the stable. Tess spat out the feathers.

"Let that be a lesson to you! Leave my brother alone, or I will eat you next time." Tess growled at the bird watching her and it nodded quickly. The swallows learned fast and the word soon spread amongst the nesting birds that the game of chase was over. It was just as well, as they were all brooding eggs and had no time for games with doggies.

It was late summer when Mum brought one of her horses out and shouted for the children. Brogan eyed the pair as they bounded towards him, respectful of his space. "Right, you two, listen to me." They stared wide-eyed, excitement building. "Jook often told me about Bruja, who trained him up on how to hack. He in turn trained me, and now it is my turn to train you." Licking their lips, their mouths wide in a doggie grin, the puppies nodded. This sounded like fun! "So, when Mum calls you, it is your job to follow. Now, I prefer if I can see you, so stay in front, but remember, I'm in charge, so you keep out of my way because I won't stop, understand?"

"Yes, sir!" they both said as Mum climbed onto Brogan's back and called them to follow. This was the best thing ever! Well, almost – agility was still top of the list.

Mum and Dad had often taken the dogs for a walk into the country park, which they could access directly from their land. Jook had been too old to go far, but in the mornings whilst Jook had been dozing, she would take Tag and Tess out for a long walk. The park was even better than the small woodland next to the yard. The pathways they followed were used by many others;

humans, dogs, deer, badgers, foxes, squirrels, and a myriad of small creatures that they knew by scent but had never seen. There was always something new to sniff out and other dogs would leave scent messages too, like writing on a wall, telling others about themselves or what was happening.

Brogan would walk at first as they ran ahead and past him. Tess was so preoccupied sniffing the scent messages that often Brogan was beside her before she noticed. Mum would shout sternly for her to get ahead, so she would run to catch up with Tag, who was having the best time ever being in charge and leading the way. Brogan would shake his head at Tess if she lingered. "Get ahead of me, doggie. I need to see where you are, or there will be trouble." Tess would reluctantly do as she was told, but it did annoy her that she was being bossed by a horse. One day, she learned to her cost why she needed to be ahead.

They were walking up a small slope and Tess, as ever, had her nose buried into the soil just at the side of the track as Brogan came thundering along. He was watching her, but she just wouldn't move.

"TESS!" shouted Morag, "GET OUT THE WAY!" Tess looked up at the last minute as Brogan stepped on her paw.

"AAAAAAAWWWWWW," she yelped as her foot was pushed into the thankfully soft soil. Brogan fortunately didn't have any shoes on, so the damage was minimal.

Tess was yelping and holding up her sore foot, looking plaintively at Mum. Morag thought carefully; if she made a fuss of things, Tess would milk the situation, but if she acted normally and observed how Tess went then hopefully there would be no broken bones.

"Well, you were told! Now get on with you." Morag watched as Tess limped ahead feeling very sorry for herself. Tag came running back to see what all the fuss was about.

"Are you OK?" He looked at Tess, who was still limping.

"Brogan stood on my foot," she said, looking for sympathy.

"You should've stayed out of his way. You know better than to get under a horse's feet," said Tag as he turned round, "Come on, you won't believe the scent I've just picked up." Tess sulkily walked faster.

As Tag's enthusiasm filtered through, she forgot about her sore paw and started to run after him. By the end of the hack, she didn't feel sore at all and had learned an important lesson about horses.

The summer days were beginning to grow shorter; autumn was on its way. The puppies were strong and fit with their agility and hacking walks. Life was good. In the evenings, they would lay beneath Mum and Dad, their heads and paws resting on the humans' feet.

It was late autumn when they had their first big adventure. Mum opened the boot of the car, which could only mean one thing – agility! They both bounded into the back as Mum put their leads and two bowls in the boot with them. Tess sniffed the empty bowls and looked quizzically at Tag, who was far too busy panting with excitement, a small whine in his throat. The door closed and Mum got in the car, starting the engine as Tess and Tag stared out of the back window, their noses leaving wet streaks on the glass. This time they were going somewhere different; they were going to their first competition.

The journey was far longer than they had ever experienced before, and they took it in turns to lie and rest whilst the other kept lookout. Mum had opened a window and they could catch new scents on the cool breeze floating back to them; it was really exciting! Eventually, the car pulled into a strange new place. It smelled of horses and dogs; it was wonderful. Mum got out and shut the door, telling them both to stay put whilst she got their numbers and registered them for their first Grade One class. Tess and Tag watched her go into a building, their gazes focused as they held their breaths, wondering when she would be back. Tag saw Mum first and gave an excited yelp, which Tess backed up with a sharp bark.

"Right, children…" said Mum as she opened the boot, "Wait." They both obediently sat and waited for their leads to be put on, but it was very difficult. Now they could really smell all the wonderful scents and hear all the excited dogs shouting encouragement to each other – this was just the best thing ever!

Tess and Tag were only ever on leads when they were doing agility, so they tried very hard not to pull Mum as she took them into a large building where there was just so much going on; their brains were on overload.

"Hi!" Mum shouted out to the humans and dogs the children recognised from their training sessions.

"Hoy! Hoy!" shouted Tag, "What is this place?"

"Calm down, son. This is a show, isn't it great?" Hoy grinned as he stared at one of the three rings that had been set up in the arena. There was a course of jumps, a tunnel, weaves, an A-frame, a dog walk, and a seesaw. "Now, when it's your turn to go, you really need to listen to the instructions from your human. This is the real deal, kids. This is what we train for." Tess and Tag were panting with excitement. Mum passed Tess's lead to Hoy's human. "Looks like Tag is going first, kiddo. We can watch from here." Tess was beside herself with frustration; it was always Tag first, it just wasn't fair. She yowled and yelped as she saw Mum go into the ring with Tag.

"Sit," Mum said firmly, "Wait." Tag was trembling with excitement, but he always tried so hard to be a good boy so he waited, watching intently, his tongue lolling out in a frantic pant. "Go!" The magic word! He shot off like a bullet for the first fence as Mum ran as fast as she could to keep up. "Left!" He spun in the air around the wing of the fence. "Go!" He jumped the next row of fences. "Tunnel, tunnel, tunnel!" Looking up, he saw the entrance to the nearest tunnel. He loved tunnels – they were great fun and he sped through it, nearly knocking it over with his speed. Bursting out of the end, he searched for Mum's next command, his eyes already fixed on the nearest jump.

"Go!" That meant go straight on. "Right!" Round he went. "HERE," Mum shouted sternly, both her arms parallel and pointing to the ground; that meant go between two jumps. Mum swung her left hand up. "Go." Tag twisted to the left and took the fence at an angle. "A-frame." His legs were pumping, his claws gripping the surface as he leapt onto the wooden A-frame, making sure he went on at the very bottom, scrambling up to the top. Even though he could confidently jump down from there, he knew he had to go to the very bottom and wait. "Touch!" There was the command and he paused, his mouth gaping in an enormous smile. "Go." Off to the next fence, sharp turn right, another fence, then there they were – the weave poles.

"Weeeeeave," Mum shouted. Tag loved the weave poles. He threaded himself through at an unbelievable speed, not missing one. "Dog walk." Onto the narrow plank that slopped up to a longer plank barely wide enough for two paws and down the other side, waiting once more. "Touch." Mum ran past, two more fences jumped, then, "Seesaw." This was the hardest one. Tag scrambled up the plank so fast it barely had time to tip down as he ran along the other side. It just touched the ground in time. "Go, go, go!" That meant run as fast as you can and jump all the fences in front of you. Tag was a blur and as he ran through the finish line, then everyone cheered. He turned to see Mum laughing and smiling at him. "Good boy, good boy, where's mummy's good boy?" Tag's heart swelled with pride. Mum was pleased – he had been a very good boy. His special toy was given to him, which was only played with at agility. He shook it from side to side in sheer joy.

"Did you see me? Did you see me?" he shouted excitedly to Tess as she scowled at him, trying not to be jealous that he went first. She nodded and stared at Mum, yelping loudly.

"My turn, my turn!" Mum took her lead and passed Tag's to Hoy's human as she led Tess to join the line of dogs waiting for their turn at the ring. She couldn't contain her excitement, a strange whimpering yowl escaping through her lips as she watched the other dogs run the course. Tess knew she wasn't as fast as Tag, but she could turn tighter and she was quicker than the other dogs she had seen. Then it was her turn – it was just brilliant.

"Sit! Wait!" Mum said firmly as she walked to her starting position. Tess sat, holding one paw up, ready for the off. "Go!" Tess flew over the fence, barking in excitement as she shouted to Mum, "Where next? Where next?", her eyes shining, a huge doggy grin of excitement on her face. "Left!" Tess flew left and jumped the next three fences, barking her head off and looking over her shoulder at Mum. "Tunnel, tunnel, tunnel." She was in and out in a flash and already locked onto the fence in front. "Go!" Over she went. "Right." She was going so fast she nearly didn't hear the command. She hesitated for a second then turned.

"HERE." Through the two fences. "Go." Mum's left hand caused Tess to do an impossible sideways jump to take the fence. "A-frame." She sped forwards. Mum could trust her more than Tag to be accurate on the equipment and she neatly ran up and down the other side. Mum didn't even need to tell her to touch. "Go." Off she went over the next, still barking like a maniac, then sharp right and through the weaves. Tess always found these difficult and she knew she had to be accurate, so she slowed down slightly and did every one. "Dog walk." That was her favourite; she sped along the narrow planks as though it were on the ground. The next two fences were a blur, then the seesaw; up she went and paused in the middle, letting it tip down to make a clean exit. "Go, go, go!" There they were – the jumps in a row. She flew down them, still barking at Mum. Everyone was clapping and cheering. She could hear Tag barking and shouting "well done!" and she just couldn't have felt prouder. She looked up at Mum. "Good girl! Good girl! Where's my little princess?" Tess beamed as she took her toy and joined Tag.

They were both buzzing with excitement, so Mum took them out of the large shed and into the fresh air. A section of field had been set aside for people to exercise their dogs, but they had to stay on the lead. It was so difficult not to pull the lead from Mum's hands as it was all so very, very exciting, but they tried hard to be good, not really understanding why they weren't running round the course again. After a brisk walk around the field, they went back to the car and Mum opened the boot, letting them jump in. She sat with them in the boot, a real pack moment for Tess and Tag to just sit and watch other dogs go by with Mum. They felt so safe and happy. A bowl was filled with water and put beside them, both of their noses competing for space to lap up the cool water. There was a rustling from the front of the car as Mum fished out some dog treats as a reward for being so well behaved.

Once she was satisfied they were cool enough, the boot was closed and they had the stern command to stay. Pressing their noses against the back window, they watched as Mum disappeared into the shed again. It seemed like ages before she returned, a huge smile on her face. "Come on, you two," she said as she opened the boot and put their leads on, "You are such good babies!" She led them back into the shed where the courses were being dismantled and everyone was standing around a row of tables. Tag and Tess stood grinning their doggy grins, getting pats from Hoy's human. There was a round of applause and they watched as Mum went forwards and picked up a strange ribbon-like blob. She held it down to Tag's nose and he sniffed it politely. "Look, Tiggy Tag, you won! This is your first ever rosette!" Tag didn't know why but he knew Mum was really pleased with him. He puffed his chest out in pride. Mum was called back to the table again and returned with a similar ribbon blob. "Princess Tess, my pretty wee girly, you're second, what a good wee girl." Tess sniffed and licked the offered rosette, feeling just as proud as Tag.

The children were exhausted and lay in the boot on the way home dozing, happy and tired. They both knew they were going to love shows!

CHAPTER FIVE

Winter came again, though this time without Uncle Jook. The puppies remembered what they had been taught about the puppy bath and tried to keep their feet as clean as possible. Tag, as always, tried to be the best at keeping his feet clean and he did a really good job. Tess, however, seemed to be a mud magnet; every time she went back to the house from the yard, she would forget and run through puddles and mud, making a dip in the puppy bath essential.

Life continued in the same rhythm, with days spent outside helping Mum and Dad in the yard, guarding them as they put out the horses or mucked out. A horse yard could be a place full of danger for dogs, with tractors moving around, large bales of haylage, cars and such. Mum was always very aware of teaching the puppies that if the tractor was moving (usually driven by Dad), they had to come straight to her side and wait with her at a safe distance till it had stopped. If they couldn't see Mum, they would look for their nearest human aunty (staff member), who also knew to look out for the dogs when the tractor was moving. Dad would always say that he could see them and wouldn't run them over, but Mum knew how quickly accidents could happen. It would only take a moment's lapse of concentration and an oblivious pup for it to be game over, so Tess and Tag learned very early on to be wary of large moving vehicles and to always look for Mum or Dad, their protectors.

In the evenings, they lay in the caravan as their humans watched the noisy box with strange pictures. Sometimes Tess would look at the box and try to understand what she could see. Wildlife programmes were fun, and Mum and Dad would laugh at her as she sat at their feet staring at the television, listening to the commentary. Old Mum and Dad still came to visit regularly. They would all sit about chatting and drinking tea as Tag lent against Old Dad's leg as he gently rubbed his ears. Tag loved having his ears rubbed; it felt so good. Tess would always be with Mum listening to everyone speaking.

Once a week if the weather was good enough, Mum would take either Tess or Tag to agility training. This was one of the highlights of their week, along with going on hacks. Brogan had decided that the dogs were up to standard to hack out with him, and they loved it. Going on walks with a horse was much more fun than going on walks with a human. Horses could move much faster and Brogan specialised in a slow trot that matched the normal trot of a dog. They could go for miles like this and Tag and Tess became fit and strong, their athletic bodies burning off calories as they ran through the woodlands catching scents, chasing squirrels, and following Brogan. The best was when Brogan would start to run fast and they had to keep ahead of him so Mum could see where they were. It was really difficult, but Tess became almost as fast as Tag, and their stamina held them in good stead for the agility shows to come.

Spring came early that year, dry but cold. The horses were put out into the fields early and life got a little easier. Tag was patrolling one morning when a large raven landed on the grass ahead of him. "Hey doggie, want to play?" it cawed at him, daring him to chase. Tag was almost fully grown, his muscles strong and well developed with all the exercise. He grinned and sprinted down the grass, taking the raven by surprise. It flew straight up, cawing and laughing as Tag jumped, barking at its tail feathers. He watched with satisfaction as it flew away. Tess came trotting up to see what was going on.

"Was that the same crow from last summer?" she asked as they both wandered back, sniffing around the stables.

"Nope, it was a new one."

"How do they know about you?" she said, shaking her head in bemusement. Tag paused and considered it for a moment.

"You know what, I'm going to ask the next one I see." He trotted off with Tess close behind. Mum was standing at the hayshed.

"Look what I've got," she said, holding up a ball. Tag and Tess bounded around her, barking with excitement – it was playtime! Mum wasn't very good at throwing a ball – it never went very far – but Tess knew she had a good chance of catching it if she sneaked a little bit away from Mum and waited on the grass, giving herself a head start. Tag knew what Tess was up to, but he didn't mind letting her have a chance. They watched as Mum put the ball into a strange stick thing. "Ready?" Boy, were they ready! She flicked the stick thing and the ball flew out high in the air, heading down the grass. They were off – Tess ahead, barking and yacking in excitement, with Tag like a dragster tearing after her, overtaking just at the last second as she reached the ball, snatching it from under her nose.

"That's not fair, it's mine!" exclaimed Tess as she ran frustrated beside Tag, trying to snatch the ball from his mouth as he brought it back to Mum. He glanced at her sideways as he chewed the ball, tilting his head, pretending to let her take it, then snatching it away as her jaws snapped shut. As he reached Mum, he dropped it for her to pick up and throw again. Tess took her opportunity, picking it up and giving it a good chew before spitting it out for Mum. They could play like this all day. Dad appeared, laughing at them.

"Want Daddy to throw the ball?" he said. They both barked madly. Dad was the best at ball throwing, and with the stick thing, it was going to go a long, long way. They watched as he loaded the stick and BOOM! It was thrown all the way to the end of the yard. They raced after it, neck and neck. Tag was going so fast that he overshot, grabbing a mouthful of grass instead as he skidded to a halt. Tess finally closed her mouth around the ball first. She was so pleased, a muffled bark coming out of her stuffed mouth as she congratulated herself. Tag ran beside her, a huge grin on this face, full of good humour – he would beat her the next time. They would play like this till they were so exhausted they just couldn't run any more, then the ball would be put away for another time Life was just perfect, their pack was perfect, and the children couldn't have been happier.

One of the best things to do on a hack was to go to the river. Tag and Tess had never properly swum, but they did love to splash about in the shallows snapping at fish. Tess was especially good, holding her breath underwater as she dunked her head in, trying to grab a fish as it skittered past. It was a trick Uncle Jook had taught her. She missed Jook. Sometimes when they were hacking with Brogan they would notice him staring ahead, a strange look on his face. When they looked, Tess sometimes thought she had seen Jook's tail disappearing around a corner as she caught the faintest hint of his scent name carried in the air. She liked to think he was with them exploring in the woods as he had done as a young dog.

Spring was rapidly giving way to summer and, much to Tag's annoyance, the swallows were back. He was lying on the grass taking in the scents in the air when the first annoying little bird appeared. "Hey, doggie!" it shouted as it spun overhead, singing a strange song about faraway places. Tag turned his head and ignored the bundle of feathers now perched on the gutters of the stables staring down at him. "I said, hey doggie!" The swallow peered at Tag, who continued to look the other way. The swallow paused to consider its next daring move. It hopped off the gutter and flitted down to the rail next to Tag. "Look, let's talk." The swallow waited as Tag glanced in its direction.

"I've nothing to say to you, bird." Tag looked away again.

"Don't be like that," the swallow chirruped faster, "I was just going to call a truce."

"What's a truce?" Tag was intrigued.

"We agree not to tease you into chasing us if you agree not to eat our babies." Tag was perplexed; he had never wanted to eat baby birds. Why would they think that?

"OK, I will leave your babies alone." He looked at the little bird, who was preening its colourful feathers.

"Well now, that is a deal. Hey, I can tell you some strange stories if you like?"

"What kind of stories?" Tag was hooked.

"Stories of sand and water so wide you can't see the other side. It takes days to fly over, days of hardship, endurance and danger." The swallow took off, spiralling into the sky, singing his heart out. Tag watched him go, his mind mulling over what had been said.

The sound of a large vehicle brought him back to the present. Dad had been putting stone down for a new stable block and it looked like it was being delivered. Tag trotted over to Tess, who was standing by the caravan watching the van pull up. She tensed as her keen nose twitched from side to side.

"What is it?" Tag whispered as Mum and Dad came out to greet the men pouring out of the van.

"One of them can't be trusted. He smells wrong," she replied, her eyes fixed in a manic stare. Tag sniffed hard then, yes – he caught it too. He stalked to Mum's side as the human with the bad smell got out of the van. A low growl vibrated in Tag's throat, a clear warning not to challenge his pack leader. The man looked nervously down at Tag, a nasty glint in his eye. Mum stared at the man and gently put her hand on Tag's head.

"My dog doesn't like the way you smell," she said to the man, who was hurriedly unstrapping the webbing keeping the flatpack stable in place on the trailer. The other men looked at Morag then back at the dog standing at her side, staring at their companion. Tess had slipped to the other side and was also glaring at the man.

"Smart dog," one of them whispered.

"We'll get this unloaded here for you then." The first man tried to grin as they unstrapped the wooden boards and put them on the ground next to the caravan.

Tag looked up to Mum's face; she really understood! He grinned at her, and she smiled and ruffled his ears. Both Tess and Tag monitored the men as they unloaded then went on their way. As the van disappeared up the driveway, they looked at each other, proud as punch that they had completed their first mission as guard dogs.

Mum took them both to two shows that year and they came back with rosettes from both their classes. Tag and Tess didn't care about the rosettes; they only wanted to please Mum and have fun. To be honest, Mum didn't care about the rosettes either, so long as the dogs were happy and having the time of their lives.

All too soon, the winter came again and it was back to mud and cold, the caravan literally on its last legs. The routine was the same and this made the dogs happy and content; they knew what to expect day to day and just enjoyed being part of a pack. They had quickly learned that they seemed to have a very large human pack. There was Mum and Dad, Old Mum and Dad, the livery clients they saw once or twice a week, and the staff that were there pretty much every day. They soon learned who was allowed into the pack by watching Mum and Dad; if their body language and scent said it was OK, then everything was good.

Uncle Jook had taught them very quickly not to bark at friends and to only make a noise when something sounded different or smelt wrong. They had become very good at reading their leaders' body language and were quick to be alert if Mum or Dad looked tense. Sometimes Mum and Dad had an argument, which the babies hated. They would try to be inconspicuous and lie in their beds if voices were raised. It didn't happen often, and Mum and Dad always made friends again, but still, Tag especially hated to hear shouting. It reminded him of angry barking; he was such a gentle dog that he hated angry energy.

It was past mid-winter and the days were lengthening when the children felt a change in the energy of their pack leaders. There was an air of excitement as they watched their Dad fence off a rectangle of the big field behind the caravan and store fence posts and wire in the space. It wasn't quite spring when the men came to work on the newly fenced-off area. Tag liked them all straight away, and Tess also gave her approval to their good-natured scents. The men would play with the dogs in between working on a strange brick construction they were putting up. Mum and Dad said it was the foundations for the new house. Tag and Tess had no idea what that was, but it made Mum and Dad happy, so they were happy too.

The men finished their part of the work then more strangers came and started building the wooden structure. When the workers left for the night, Mum and Dad would walk on the planks that were the floor beams of the new house and imagine what the final build would be like. Tag and Tess would join in this fun game of balancing. They watched Mum and Dad walking along the narrow planks and copied them (they found it easier with four feet!) as they explored the strange new thing that was growing before their eyes.

Over the summer, the house grew. The children had to restrain themselves from guard duties as so many new faces would come and go, all involved in building the new house. Having grown up with heavy machinery, the dogs knew to keep out of the way and would lie in the grass to watch proceedings from the safety of the stable yard where only the liveries and horses would venture. Mum only managed to take them to one show that year, but they didn't mind – they were still hacking out with Brogan and loving life.

Summer gave way to autumn and the swallows left for exotic countries. Tag was trotting round the yard on patrol when he spied a family of crows. They were sitting on the arena fence watching him. As he drew near, he heard the almost grown chicks from this year say to what he assumed was their mama, "Is that the fast doggie?" The older bird cocked its head from side to side. "Yes, younglings, that is the fast doggie crow-catcher." The young birds made a strange cawing sound in fear. The older bird looked at Tag and winked. "If you don't behave, young birds, then fast doggie crow-catcher will eat you!" Tag smiled to himself – so he had become the terror of crow chicks! He lowered his head and growled.

"I heard that one of you had been very, very bad." The young crows flapped their wings in fright. "I might just gobble you all up." Tag sprang forwards and the birds took flight cawing, the youngsters in fear and the older bird in laughter. It circled overhead.

"Fast doggie nearly caught me!" It landed on the arena fence again. "It was my grandfather you caught that day, fast doggie. I thank you for sparing his life. You are always remembered in the roosts, and stories are passed onto the next generation." Tag sat down and puffed his chest out with pride.

"I am honoured, crow. I will always chase but never catch again." The crow bowed and took flight.

"Don't tell the youngsters that!" Tag watched as it flew away laughing.

Tess wandered up and stared at the bird in the sky. "They are just weird," she said, snorting and wiping her face with her paw. "Want to explore what's been built today?" Without waiting for a reply, she spun round. "Race you!"

"That's not fair!" shouted Tag as he easily caught up and overtook her.

It looked more and more like a proper den (Mum and Dad called it a house) now that all the walls and most of the roof were on. They wandered through the rooms balancing on the beams as Mum and Dad talked about what was to go where. It was a great game. Tag and Tess had become very good beam balancers and they grinned their wide doggie grins, tongues lolling, eyes shining with joy as they played in the wooden building with their pack.

It was almost mid-winter when the house was finished and everyone was settled in. Old Mum and Dad had come to join the pack permanently, much to the delight of the puppies. Extra pets and fussing were dished out, and treats were sometimes sneaked to them when Mum and Dad weren't looking. The old caravan was finally towed away to be scrapped; it was tired and done and ready to go, but everyone watched sadly as it rattled its way up the track on its final journey. However, the new house was so much warmer with central heating and not a simple oil-filled radiator, and at first, Tag and Tess found it almost too warm. They were tough yard dogs and used to the cold. Their first beds were in the back kitchen on the cool linoleum, but curled up in their new beds, they were still content and happy with life.

Work on the yard continued as normal throughout that winter. Once more, the days changed and the sun stayed longer in the sky. Now fully grown, the puppies were coming into their full strength. Mum still found time to take them to competitions and Tag especially was gaining a reputation as an extremely fast dog. He didn't care; he just loved to run and jump and to please Mum. Tess was just as delighted and practised making impossible turns in the air to catch up time as her legs just couldn't match

Tag's speed. Every week the highlight would be practice sessions in the sectioned-off area of the field with all of the agility equipment. They loved it and they loved their doggie friends, who would come along and share gossip and news from outside the yard.

At first, Tag and Tess were a bit shy. Their lives didn't change much; they guarded the yard and went out on hacks with the horses, whereas the other dogs seemed to go to many different places and do lots of different things. The others would listen to Tess tell stories of their hacks, how they had had to run fast to keep up with the horses, and how they would see the scent stories of all the animals in the woodlands. She was a very good storyteller and everyone was amazed at what they had done. This made the children feel a bit better and content with their lives.

Over the summer, there was work going on inside the new house. Mum and Dad were making a bedroom and living space upstairs in what had been the roof; now it had a staircase leading up and this was a new experience for the children. Because of their knowledge of the agility equipment, it didn't take them long to work out how to go up and down the stairs. They were so excited with this new plaything, especially when Mum and Dad played hide and seek. Dad would hold them as Mum ran away and hid (they did this in the yard, but it was more of a challenge in the house), then Dad would let them go and they had to find Mum; she was brilliant at hiding.

Tess would use her clever nose, trying to find the scent that was the strongest and most recent; it wasn't always easy as there were so many strong scents of their pack in the house, but she was usually very good at narrowing down which room Mum might be in. Tag used his eyesight; he ran like a maniac, always trying to be first, and often missed a clue that Tess with her steadier pace would pick up. They would stand and listen, trying to hear Mum giggle or whisper their names to give them a clue. Sometimes she hid so well that she had to speak loudly so they would find her, jumping around and barking madly with laughter at this wonderful game. They loved playing with Mum and Dad; they always had time for them.

Once the upstairs had been built and the new living room was in, with a huge widow from ceiling to floor that looked out over the yard, well, the children absolutely loved it. The best thing was in the evening when Mum and Dad were watching TV and they would allow Tag and Tess to jump up and cuddle into them on their chairs. Tag would sit with Dad and Tess with Mum. Tag would sometimes beat Tess to Mum's lap, where he would sit and look at Tess with a glint in his eye as she stared at him sulkily from Dad's chair. Eventually, he would give in and step over, allowing Tess to swap with him. They loved their evening cuddles, trying to stay as long as possible. When they eventually got too hot, they would jump down and lie on their own big doggie cushions at Mum and Dad's feet. The best bit, though, was when they were given the privileged position of sleeping in the bedroom beside Mum and Dad's bed. Life was wonderful, it was perfect, but it was about to change.

CHAPTER SIX

Another winter had started. The routine was the same and all seemed well. There was the usual strange celebration that happened halfway through the winter, which the puppies loved. They got to see more of the pack, wear tinsel on their collars, and sometimes have paper hats balanced on their heads – it was a great game. They even got special treats and rewards, and everyone was happy, which made them happy. Not long after the celebration, Tess and Tag noticed a change in their humans. There was fear and anxiety; something was wrong. They did their best to cheer up their leaders, trying really hard to be especially obedient, but one night, Mum and Dad left and one of the 'uncles' (a member of staff) fed them and took them out on the night run.

It was very early in the morning that the children heard their mum and dad's car return. Sleepily, they greeted them at the door, wondering where they had been, but the scents they could detect were upsetting. Tag and Tess could smell the faint scent they dreaded the most; death. One of the aunties of the pack was with them and everyone had been crying. Tess pushed her nose into Mum's hand to reassure her, but there was no response.

"Tess, come here and lie down. We can't help. We just need to be good and quiet." Tag pushed Tess away and took her into the living room where they lay under the table, watching the doorway anxiously. They saw everyone move into Old Mum and Dad's side of the house; there was some talking, then crying. Crying! The puppies couldn't help themselves; their pack was upset and something was making them very sad. They trotted into the room and watched as Old Mum and Dad sat distraught, comforted by Aunty, Mum, and Dad. Tag let out a small whine and went over to Old Dad, pushing his head into his hands, trying desperately to make him feel better. Tess was unsure; she looked at her pack leaders and their faces mirrored the grief she could smell. Mum put out her hand and Tess tucked her head under and pressed against her leg, trying to comfort Mum but not knowing what was wrong.

The following day, something happened that would change Tag and Tess's lives forever. Mum and Dad left early. Everyone was sad and quiet, so the children slipped out into the yard and stayed with the yard staff as they went about their duties. A few hours had passed when they heard the familiar sound of the car returning. Trotting up to greet their mum and dad, hoping that a good pack welcome would make them happy once more, they stopped in their tracks as Dad opened the door and stepped out. He was carrying something. Carefully, he put his tiny bundle on the ground and the children stared at the smallest dog they had ever seen.

"I'm Skye, I'm Skye!" the small dog shouted out, full of false bravado as Tess and Tag could smell the fear and grief inside of her. "I'm in charge, I'm in charge!" She puffed her chest out and tried to stand as tall as she could as the other dogs towered over her, her small tail wagging furiously as she tried to make friends.

Tag sniffed her thoroughly; he could tell she was malnourished. She didn't smell healthy; her body was weak and her legs slightly deformed. Tess slowly curled up one lip as she regarded the small dog in front of her.

"I think you will find, Skye, that you are very much not in charge." She sniffed Skye coolly and looked up at Mum and Dad. "I hope this thing isn't staying?" she said, hoping that they understood her.

"Now, Tess," Mum patted her head, "This is your new wee cousin, Skye. She is going to live with us now, so be nice." Skye tugged at the lead she was on, desperate to get out and run about, the fear inside of her making her frantic. She had been top dog with her last dad, but he was ill. She had tried to make him better, tried to be good, but sometimes she couldn't help but be naughty. She had so much energy, but he could no longer walk her.

The previous night, something terrible had happened; her dad had been very sick and had laid down on the bedroom floor. Skye had barked and barked to try to get help, but no one had come. She had lain beside him as she felt him slowly start to slip away and a strange scent filled her nose; she hadn't liked it. Then, as she had been about to give up hope, someone came. She had known the human before, but there were two others with her that she hadn't recognised. The first human had locked her in a room downstairs away from her dad. Then one of the strangers had come in and tried to comfort her. Skye had been frantic. She had run around the room at top speed, stopping every so often to peer into the face in front of her as she tried to tell her that her dad was in trouble. Finally, the stranger had put a lead on her and taken her next door to the neighbours she had met a few times. There she had stayed, not knowing where her dad was or when he would come back.

The next morning, the strangers had come back for her. They were very, very sad. They wrapped her up in a jacket that smelled of her dad and took her away in a car to this place.

Tess wasn't happy; she sensed this small annoyance of a dog was going to stay and no one had consulted her! Dropping her head, she sloped off in a sulk, leaving Tag standing awkwardly looking at Skye, his tail slowly wafting side to side as he tried to be welcoming. He could smell that Skye was afraid and tried to sound fierce to hide his own fear.

"Hi, Skye, I'm Tag and that's Tess." He glanced towards the rear end of Tess as she disappeared into the house. "She is in charge when it comes to making important decisions. I am the guard dog of the yard, so you must find your place in this pack."

"What is a pack?" Skye followed the humans towards the house, pulling on the lead (she hadn't been walked very often). Tag looked down at her.

"We are dogs, they are humans. They are our leaders and together our family is called a pack. Each pack member has their place and duties." They went inside. Skye was quiet as she thought about what Tag had said.

"Why are you in here?" growled Tess as she glared at Skye.

"Now Tess, NO! This is Skye, she is part of the family now and we have to look after her." Tess dropped her ears and lowered her head submissively as Mum gave her into trouble.

Skye trotted everywhere, searching around the house, trying to understand where she was. There was a bed in a cage in the back kitchen and the humans had placed the jacket with her dad's scent into it. Skye knew that this was to be her bed, but it was strange. In her last home, she had slept where she pleased. She trotted back into the living room where Tag and Tess were lying.

"Where is your pack?" asked Tess, half hoping they would come back for Skye soon. The small dog sat down, her eyes shifting nervously, her body tense with fear.

"I don't know. My dad fell asleep and I couldn't wake him up." Skye licked her lips and stood up again. Unable to sit still, she trotted back into the kitchen to check the jacket was still there. Tag and Tess looked at each other; they had smelled the scent of death on Mum and Dad last night and they could smell it also on Skye, but it had been faint. The scent did not belong to them; it was from another.

"Do you think her dad is dead?" said Tag softly to Tess. She sniffed and felt her heart soften a little in sympathy.

"Maybe, but that's not our fault."

"Tess…" said Tag gently, "Remember, Uncle Jook was not asked if we should come and stay here." He lay down and watched Skye trot around the main kitchen nervously, panting and stressed as the humans spoke with each other. Tess sighed; he was right.

"Well, she can stay, I suppose, but she is not in charge, no matter what she thinks." Tess looked at Skye as she trotted back into the room. "You can stay, Skye, but do as we tell you." Skye sat down and stared defiantly at the two dogs.

"I don't want to stay! I want my dad! I want to go home!" Her small heart was breaking. She couldn't understand what had happened and why she was here. Tess glanced at Tag and he raised his eyebrows. Skye was obviously much younger than they were; she sounded not much more than a puppy. Tess sighed.

"That smell you have on you…" Tess paused to see

if Skye understood. The small dog blinked and nodded. "Was that the smell on your dad when he fell asleep?"

"Yes, it was strange. I didn't like it."

"Skye, that smell is the smell of death," said Tess.

"What's death?" asked Skye, confused. Tag stood up and gave Skye a good sniff of reassurance.

"Death, Skye, is when someone falls asleep and never wakes up. They leave their bodies behind and go somewhere else."

"Where do they go? When do they come back?" asked Skye, her fear deep.

"They never come back in their bodies, but sometimes you will catch their scent faintly on the wind or see them standing, watching, just for a moment as they visit. Then they go back to the other place," continued Tag. Skye dropped her head and lay down, anguish and sorrow filling her. She was alone.

"Where is the other place? How do I get there to find my dad?" she said.

"We don't know, but one day we will go there, all of us, and you will be with him again." Tag had done his best. He looked at Tess and she relented.

"You are not alone now, Skye, you will be part of our pack and we will teach you how to be a good dog." Tess tried to sound welcoming, but she still was not happy about the whole situation. Skye looked up at the two huge dogs towering above her.

"But I was in charge, I had to look after Dad and now he has left me behind. Was I a bad dog?"

"I am sure you did the best you could. We will teach you how to be better." Tess raised her head in a haughty glance. "First of all, learn the rules. Tag is first, I am second, and you…" she glowered at Skye, "are last. This applies to all things. If you follow us, we will teach you."

"Always, always do as Mum and Dad tell you, never question them and always obey them. That way, they will keep you safe," finished Tag.

Skye looked sadly at the ground. She didn't like this one little bit.

That first night was the hardest for Skye, locked in the puppy cage with only her dad's jacket for comfort. Despite her exhaustion, she lay awake for a long, long time listening to the different sounds of the house and picking up the scents of her new family. Skye had never been taught to go to the toilet outside; she had just messed in the house and her dad would clear it up. Now, though, she struggled to hold it in, unwilling to wet her bed.

It was early the next morning when she heard the humans get up and the one Tag and Tess called Mum came into the kitchen. Skye jumped up at the cage door, desperate to get out. Mum opened the door to the outside first then opened the cage door, expecting Skye to run outside to go to the toilet, but Skye didn't understand. She simply let out a flood onto the kitchen floor.

"NO!" shouted Mum as she grabbed Skye and almost threw her out the door. Cowering in confusion, Skye continued to urinate on the decking, wanting to run away but too frightened to move. Tess came in and looked at the wet floor in disgust.

"We do the toilet outside on the grass, NEVER in the house!" She curled her lip at Skye, who despite having already flooded everywhere still wet herself again. "This way." Tess pushed past her and trotted down the ramp, stopping at the bottom to pee. "See, like this." Skye watched with confusion and trotted after her.

Tag brought up the rear, glancing at the wet floor that Mum was mopping up. "She messed in the house," said Tess. Tag stared at her in shock and Skye shrank with humiliation. "You have a lot to learn," said Tag, "Follow us." He set off on his morning patrol, which started with his favourite toilet area. Skye followed the big dogs and learned how and where to go to the toilet like a proper dog.

The first months of Skye's arrival were difficult for everyone. Tag felt like he had to referee between Tess and Skye all the time, and for such a gentle dog like Tag, it was very taxing. Even their human mum and dad were finding that Skye knew nothing about being a dog. She messed in the house because she didn't know how to hold on or ask to get out. She constantly tried to pick fights with Tag and Tess, clearly trying to be in charge but obviously too unsure of herself to be a reliable leader. On more than one occasion, Tess lost her temper with her so much that she actually grabbed her and tried to shake her like a rag doll. Mum would break up the fight and Tess would try to walk away, but Skye would fly back at her and start the fight all over again. She was a typical terrier.

They all tried to include her in pack activities, like going for a walk in the woods. Mum didn't take her along with the horses because she was so small and had no horse sense at all; it would have ended in tears and tragedy. So instead, Mum would walk with everyone along the leafy lane to the park, but even this was hard. She had to keep Skye on a lead because they would only get halfway to the park and Skye would turn round and run back to the house. She just didn't seem to want to join in.

One night, Mum and Dad were watching TV while Tag and Tess lay on their cushions in front of their chairs. The living room was upstairs and it was late at night, the only light coming from the TV. Skye was sitting beside Tag's cushion; she had wanted to sit up on the chairs with the humans, but she had been relegated to only being allowed to sit near the other dogs. It had taken the humans a few weeks to figure out that by allowing Skye up onto the chairs for a cuddle when they felt so sorry for her, it was making it harder for her to integrate into the pack. They were inadvertently raising her status by allowing her to sit with them above Tag and Tess and this was why Skye kept picking fights, now that she was going through the painful process of being bottom dog all the time.

Everyone was still. Skye sat looking at this group of humans and dogs she had never asked to be associated with. Her small heart ached at the loss of her own human dad and she tried to understand what Tag had told her about death. As she sat, a familiar scent drifted up the stairwell. Skye stood up, alert, her head shoved through the banister railings as she stared into the darkness of the stairs, the scent growing stronger. Her little tail wagged furiously; it was her dad! Tag looked at Tess, who sat up slightly and stared at Mum. The two humans had noticed Skye and were watching her, looking at the stairs. Both dogs watched; they could see the strange, faint image of a man hovering on the stairs eye to eye with Skye, smiling at her.

"Dad! Dad! You've come back!" Skye's tail continued to wag as she tracked the image she could see as it hovered in the darkness. The man slowly shook his head; even Skye knew that meant no.

"Sssstay." The faint whisper of the words could barely be heard by the dogs and not at all by the humans, who couldn't even see the figure floating in front of them. Skye sat down, a faint whine in her throat. "N-n-new family." The faint words drifted into their ears and Skye felt dejected; her dad would not be coming back for her; he wanted her to stay here. "B-b-be g-g-good." The figure started to fade and float back down the stairs, Skye watching it all the way till it was gone.

Tag looked at the small, lost dog with her head jammed through the railings. "Now you know," he said, feeling sorry for her, "You must do as he says, stay here and be good."

"I don't know how to be good. Everything I do is wrong and I get shouted at. I don't understand." Skye lay down, her nose in her paws and her eyes closed.

"Then you should pay attention." Tess snapped. Tag looked at her sternly.

"Well, one thing that I know annoys everyone is you barking," said Tag.

"My dad told me to bark at every noise I hear. I was his guard," said Skye defiantly.

"Well, your dad is gone now, so you need to learn." Tess closed her eyes, bored of this conversation. She drifted off to sleep and started to snore softly. The TV mumbled away and the humans shrugged off the strange incident.

"I am the guard dog here. If I don't bark, then you don't bark." Tag said firmly.

"The humans join in with my barking." Skye opened her eyes and glared at Tag.

"They aren't joining in; they are telling you off," he continued.

"Sounds like barking to me." Skye didn't know why she was being argumentative; she was just so upset as she truly thought her dad had come back to take her home. Now she knew she was never going home and she would have to make the best of it. Tag shook his head slowly, not sure if he was ever going to get through to this little dog.

CHAPTER SEVEN

To say Skye learned how to behave would be stretching the truth. She did try very hard, but she had a terrier 'never give up' attitude and was convinced that she was as good a guard dog as Tag. When Mum and Dad played with them all and threw the ball, Skye was more interested in barking in Tag or Tess's ears as they ran, never even noticing the ball they were chasing. The game would come to an end when Tess's patience gave in and she would fight with Skye, which Mum inevitably broke up.

It was worse in the house. Because she was so small, she had taken to lying unnoticed under Old Dad's chair whilst he was eating or reading, and the slightest sound would cause her to erupt in loud frenzied barking, causing Old Dad to jump in fright and make everyone shout at her to 'shut up!' Finally, Mum got fed up with it and bought an anti-bark collar. It was supposed to spray citronella into the dog's face when they barked beyond a certain volume, and it did work for a short while. The trouble was it took Skye so long to realise that it was her barking that was causing the spray that the unit would either run out of batteries or out of spray, and would click harmlessly as Skye manically shouted at the top of her voice.

There was some success. The trouble was she just couldn't help herself. She knew she would get into trouble for barking, so if she heard a noise, she would quickly run upstairs out of reach but still bark continuously. The whole family was at their wits' end with her. It was hard not to laugh, though, especially when the dogs were all out in the yard. There would be Skye running frantically behind the other dogs, trying to keep up like some manic citronella-powered steam train, clouds of vapour rising in puffs around her head as she ran barking right through the middle of it all. Eventually, they just gave up. It became normal in the household for the phrase 'Skye, shut the hell up!' to be screeched as someone knocked on the door or made a noise like a door opening.

Tess, of course, treated Skye with minimum tolerance, but occasionally they would call a truce. There were rare days when even Tess would feel sorry for her small cousin, who just didn't seem to belong. She would play-bow in front of her and ask, "Want to play chase?" Skye would wag her tail furiously. "Yes, please!" Then they would take off and roughhouse with each other, playing like good friends. Tag would watch on, his mind ticking over more serious matters of guarding. He had taken to going into Old Mum and Dad's part of the house and sitting beside Old Dad. There was a deep sadness inside Old Dad, a grief that would not go away, and sometimes it was stronger when he looked at Skye. Tag would do his best to comfort Old Dad, but he knew that even he could not fix his broken heart.

It was a special treat to be allowed into Old Mum and Dad's rooms, and it was such fun. They had a huge patio door which meant the children could all lie comfortably looking out onto the yard, watching the world go by. They each had their spot and they called it 'doggie TV'. It was during one of these moments that Tess caught the faint hint of a familiar dreaded scent coming from Old Dad. She lay and twitched her nose, studying him as he sat staring out of the patio doors. Slowly getting up, she went to his side and lay down next to him, laying her head on his feet. Tag looked at her then at Old Dad; he sensed it too. Strangely, Skye was silent for a moment, her nose also twitching, then she got up abruptly and stormed out of the room, taking herself upstairs to her bed. She lay there with a strange mix of emotions churning inside of her.

The summer passed and winter came again. Mum and Dad had bought special fleece coats for all the dogs as they were now middle-aged and needed extra heat in the snowy weather, especially Skye as she was so close to the ground. Although mature dogs, the children didn't feel old; they were still strong and active, regularly competing in agility as well as training. They were very fit, still hacking for miles with the horses. They had given up trying to get Skye to go with them. She seemed afraid to leave the comfort of the yard.

When summer came around that year, they all went

on their first holiday with their mum and dad. Tess and Tag were piled into the car, Skye watching them from the patio doors. At first, they thought they were going to a show, but Dad never came to shows with them, so they knew it was going to be a great puppy adventure. As they drove out of the yard staring out of the back window of the car, they watched Skye sadly staring back, feeling left out and unwanted. Tess, of course, didn't care; this was how it should be, how it had always been, just the children and their humans. Tag felt a pang of guilt, but he was quickly carried away with Tess's enthusiasm.

It was a very long car ride and they stopped by the side of a loch to stretch their legs. Tag and Tess had never been taught to swim properly and Mum and Dad had brought special toys that floated; they were determined that the babies discovered how much fun swimming was. It took a while to convince the children that the cold water was indeed fun to splash and play in, and to everyone's surprise, it was Tess who first paddled out of her depth and discovered that if she franticly waved her legs, she could float and move about the water. Tag took much longer to brave the swim, and when he did, there was quite a lot of splashing and panicking on his part till he felt the ground under this feet. With lots of laughter and encouragement from their mum and dad, they were gaining confidence by the minute.

Finally, they were called back to the shore, shivering

with the cold but excited by this new game they had found. Mum and Dad dried them with towels then put on special fleece coats Mum had bought just for this holiday, their front legs shoved through sleeves like a jumper. The fleece kept their bodies warm while their coats dried and they jumped into the back of the car, lying on the fleece mat, exhausted and content.

It was almost night when they arrived at their destination, having stopped twice more for toilet breaks for humans and dogs. They were staying in a dog-friendly B&B on the Isle of Skye, and it was one of the best holidays they ever had. Their days were spent going on walks in the hills and snuggled up by the fire at night. One day, they went on an extra-long journey to one of the most amazing places they had ever been to – it was called Coral Beach. The pure white pristine sand and the blue azure sea looked like something out of a tropical island, but the cold wind and sharp air were most definitely Scottish. This was the best place for the babies to perfect their swimming techniques. They would spend hours running up and down the shoreline, diving into the ocean to fetch a stick or a floating toy and bring it back. By now, Tag was up to speed with this swimming thing and his long powerful legs often got him to the prize before Tess, who would try to bark and swim at the same time. As Tag turned for home, she would grab the end of the stick, growling in frustration, and they would both bring it back to shore. It was the best fun ever.

All too soon, their holiday was over and it was time to go home, but it had convinced Mum and Dad that taking the babies on holiday was a great idea. The trip home was just as fun with Tag and Tess playing 'guess where we are' as they began to recognise their surroundings the closer to home they got. Both of them jammed their noses through the small gap in the window and sucked in lungsful of air, picking up familiar scents, excitement building as they approached their pack territory. Neither could suppress the whines filtering through their lips as they pulled into the yard, Skye running frantically towards them as they leapt out of the car, a barking session all round as they greeted each other.

"Where have you been?" exclaimed Skye as she ran round them in circles, yapping at an annoying pitch.

"It was an adventure!" Tag grinned, "We learned how to swim and chase sticks that float."

"There were lots of walks and fun. It was great!" finished Tess.

Skye quietened down and looked a little sad. "Can I come too next time?"

Tess paused and looked at her, a strange feeling in her heart; she actually felt sorry for Skye. "Why not. I can discipline you anywhere." Skye bounded past her, eagerly awaiting the next holiday.

Later that summer, the three dogs bounded out of the house first thing in the morning to start their normal patrol of the yard when they were stopped in their tracks by a new scent. Tess twitched her nose and tried to analyse the source. Skye was at her side – she had a very sharp nose as well – and even Tag could smell the strange animals. They walked over to the door of the small house that provided the staff with accommodation and sniffed at the threshold. Yes, it was definitely coming from the small house.

As the three of them stood pondering what it could possibly be, David opened the door and gently pushed them away. "No, no, you know you're not allowed." They politely stepped back and tried to peer past him. Two strange voices mewed from the back of the house. All day, they would take turns to wander over to the small house and check to see if the animals were still there, but it wasn't for another few weeks that they discovered who the scent belonged to.

Tag lay stretched out in the warm sun, the grass feeling cool beneath him. Tess was lying beside him, sitting up and surveying the air with her nose. Skye, as always, was busy hunting for moles. She was obsessed with them. One day, Mama had shown her a dead mole that had been caught in a trap and Skye immediately latched onto the small furry body with the strong smell and nasty taste. Mum had laughed and made it a game for her, thus triggering the natural hunting instincts that all Jack Russell terriers have. From that day onwards, Skye would patrol from mound of earth to mound of earth, trying to catch a live mole as it was pushing up the soil. She could even hear them tunnelling away beneath her; it was most frustrating.

Even though Tag was lying on his side, his keen eyesight caught the slinking movement as two grey low-slung animals cautiously crept along the side of the small house and beneath the tractor. He cocked his ears and sat up, staring. Tess looked round.

"What is it?"

"I don't know. I think it is the new smell animals."

Tess sniffed the air and caught the scent as the two figures darted across the yard into the hayshed. A growl built in Tag's throat and he leapt into action. Tess followed behind, yapping an alarm. Skye was last to pick up the warning but soon caught up with them, wondering what it was all about. They stopped at the bottom of the large round haylage bale and looked up at two sets of glowing yellow eyes. One set was surrounded by grey fluffy fur and the other by blue-grey smooth velvet fur. The strange animals opened their mouths to reveal shining white needle-sharp predator teeth and pink tongues. A strange angry hissing noise was directed at them as their eyes glowed with fury.

"NO!" The stern voice of Mum stopped them in their

barking. "Leave them alone!" They all turned to stare at their pack leader. What did she mean, 'leave them alone'? Surely they were intruders? "Be nice." Mum walked over to the bale and stood beside the small furry balls of fury. "This is Frankie and Benny. They are the new yard cats."

Cats. The dogs looked at each other in confusion; this was a new animal to them and they didn't like the way they smelled. The eyes continued to glare at them, but at least the hissing had stopped. Tag feigned disinterest and walked away. Tess gave them one last glare and joined him, but Skye stayed where she was, frantically wagging her tail. Here were two animals almost the same size as her; maybe they would be her friends!

"Hi, I'm Skye." She looked over her shoulder to make sure the other two were out of earshot. "I'm in charge." Benny, the smooth blue-grey cat, snorted in derision.

"I think you will find, smelly dog, that we are in charge around here." He glanced at Frankie. "We don't appreciate your kind being around. You make too much noise and scare away our prey." She began to lick her paws with disdain.

"I can hunt!" Skye blurted out. The two cats laughed in her face.

"What can you hunt? Squeaky toys, a ball perhaps." Skye felt her anger rise.

"I hunt moles." She turned and walked away. "I don't want to be your friend."

"Good!" was the parting shot.

So began the lifelong animosity between the yard cats and the yard dogs. Tag and Tess were obedient, so when they were told not to hurt the cats, they didn't, but if the cats chose to run, Tag simply couldn't resist chasing them with a furious growl in his throat. They were so arrogant, and to be honest, he found them cruel. The dogs had never had to hunt for food, so they struggled to understand the pleasure the cats found in hunting and eating their prey. They were good at it too. Mice, voles, all varieties of small birds, rabbits and even squirrels were fair game to this pair of ferocious predators.

The summer quickly gave way to autumn then another wet winter. Life continued as it had always done, only this time the dogs had to put up with sneering comments from Frankie and Benny whenever their paths crossed. To their credit, they never retaliated. For Skye, it was an opportunity to be welcomed into the dog pack – three against two, so to speak. This didn't mean that Skye and Tess were close friends, but at least she tolerated her. Unfortunately, Skye wasn't very smart when it came to trying to move up the pecking order. She would give Tess cheek and challenge her every so often, which would result in her being promptly put in her place with a snarling pin from Tess, her teeth around Skye's throat. The cats thought this was hilarious and conspired to encourage Skye to become the pack leader.

Spring arrived early that year and the swallows were back. This was the first time they met the cats and they were horrified to see the slinking shapes creeping around the yard. Tag was on patrol one morning when a swallow swooped past his head.

"Hey, doggie!" Tag muttered to himself and glanced at the circling bird.

"Yes?"

"What kind of show are you running here?" The bird flipped a few somersaults and circled again.

"What do you mean?"

"I mean, who allowed the bird killers on the yard? I thought we had an agreement." The swallow landed briefly on the gutter and looked at Tag with one bright black eye.

"Agreement?"

"Yes, that we would leave you alone if you didn't eat our chicks."

"I have never eaten one of your chicks," said Tag indignantly.

"No, but they will, and you are letting them." The swallow looked towards Benny, who had spied him talking to Tag and was creeping towards them. Tag looked round at the cat and then back to the bird.

"I will do my best to protect your chicks," he said solemnly. The bird snorted.

"Good luck with that!" There was a flurry of feathers

as he took off into the sky. Benny casually strolled past Tag keeping a wary eye on him, ready to leap onto a stable door if necessary.

"Sooo, you like to talk to the fast birdies, smelly dog?" Benny rubbed his head against the door, deliberately marking it with his scent. Tag stared at him coldly, one ear cocked back to hear if Mum was near enough to see him chase this arrogant cat.

"What's it to you, furball?" He growled a warning and Benny stared at him, his back arched and tail high.

"Hey, hey, calm down, just asking."

"You just leave them alone or else." Tag turned and walked away.

"Or else what?" Benny jeered then shot up the door frame in fright as Tag turned in the blink of an eye and ran at him.

"Or else you'll deal with me!" Tag finished his threat with a snap of his jaws and left Benny balancing on the door, staring at him in alarm.

Spring gave way to summer and the yard was busy with horses in to be trained. There was hustle and bustle everywhere from the humans doing their work and the wild animals raising their young. All the stables that had swallow nests in them had the doors kept open; this made it harder for the cats to catch the parents as they swooped in to feed their chicks. Frankie and Benny were frustrated that such tempting morsels were just out of their reach, and Tess especially took pleasure in taunting them about it.

"What's the matter, pussycats, birdies too fast for you?" she would say, strolling past them as they sunned themselves on the cabinets outside of the stables. The cats would ignore her and turn their faces away, tails twitching in annoyance.

Then one day, it happened. Benny caught a swallow. He marched onto the yard with the small bird in his mouth, absolute triumph written on his face. Tag was horrified. He could see that the bird was still alive, and Benny no doubt was going to torture it for a while. He felt the rage in him rise and he ran full pelt at Benny, who did not expect the attack. Tag knocked Benny into the stable wall with a nose punch. The cat dropped the bird as he reeled in shock.

"I told you to leave them alone!" Tag growled, standing between Benny and the swallow, who was trying to get to his feet.

"Don't you dare steal my prey!" hissed Benny as he swiped at Tag. At that moment, Mum appeared and saw the helpless bird, still shocked and on the ground.

"Benny!" she shouted "Scat!" She chased the cat off and Tag made sure he stayed away with a warning bark. He turned back to see Mum pick the bird up from the ground and gently check it for injuries; it seemed fine, just shocked. She carefully placed it in an old nest that had been abandoned and left it to recover.

As she walked away, Tag stared up at the small beak and black eyes looking down at him. "Thank you," came the hoarse whisper from the nest. "You're welcome," Tag replied. He walked away, deciding that he really didn't like cats.

That summer, Mum and Dad took the three dogs with them on holiday. They rented a small cottage up north that allowed dogs and piled everyone into the back of the car. It was the first time Skye had been in a car since she had arrived at the yard almost five years ago and it was very exciting. Tess and Tag were old hands at this and knew they were going on an adventure. They drove through rolling hills and mountains, their noses jammed against the opening at the top of the window, taking in the smells carried on the wind.

When they arrived at the small cottage, Skye tried to keep a low profile, half believing she had been taken along by accident. The three dog beds were set up in the bedroom and Skye was even more amazed; this was the first time she had been allowed to sleep with the whole pack. The honoured position of sleeping beside pack leaders was usually held by Tess and Tag, as Skye slept outside the bedroom in her own small basket, but now on holiday she was allowed to be with everyone – she felt great.

It was one of the best holidays ever. The whole time was spent exploring new places and walks. The cottage was near to a small rocky beach where Tag and Tess tried to teach Skye how to swim. She wasn't sold on the concept, preferring to run up and down barking at the others instead, but Mum would grab her and throw her in, forcing her to learn. Skye was not the best swimmer but she was very buoyant; as soon as she hit the water, she would turn and head for shore as quickly as she could. They also found some amazing walks in deep forests with gushing waterfalls.

One day, they headed out into a forest walk they had briefly explored the previous day. Mum said it looked familiar and thought that they might have been here with Jook in the past. Off they set, following the trail through wooded glades with sunbeams cascading down through the canopy, dappling the soft pine-covered path banked on one side by fern-covered purple rocks and on the other by forest. Mum took a picture of the three of them running together ahead on the path; it was the perfect shot, three dogs loving life, loving being dogs, and loving that moment in time.

They walked up and out of the woodlands, crossing a bridge onto a larger track for forestry vehicles and looping back down towards the car. Mum remembered a bridge at the bottom next to the car park where they could cross the river again, but as they neared the bridge, they saw to their dismay that it was closed for repairs. There was nothing for it; they had to turn back and retrace their steps. Fourteen miles later, they got back to the car. It was the longest walk the dogs had ever been on! All too soon, their holiday was over and it was time to head home. They lay quietly in the car, content and happy, dreaming of woodlands and rivers.

CHAPTER EIGHT

Summer gave way to autumn and winter once more. This year, Mum had only taken the children to one show, which was fine. They understood home life was so very busy. Old Mum and Dad fussed and spoiled them all, and one of the highlights of their day was being allowed into their living room to lie in front of the large patio doors where they could observe the yard in comfort. Mum and Dad said it was like doggie TV, and it pretty much was. Tag had his spot, Tess had hers, and Skye would lie cautiously close to them on her wee carpet, getting sneaky pats from Old Dad when the others were asleep.

It was during one of the sneaky patting sessions that Skye caught the scent of something she dreaded. It was faint but it was there. She looked over to Tess, knowing that her cousin had a good nose.

"Tess, Tess," she whispered.

Opening one eye, she regarded Skye coldly. "What?"

"I smell something bad."

"Your feet, perhaps?" replied Tess sarcastically, but Skye's worried face and lack of retaliation made her sit up a little and regard her. "What's wrong?" she had just asked when the faint scent drifted towards her. She looked up at Old Dad. "Oh!" she exclaimed, staring hard up into the old man's face as he watched the real television.

"Is it… is it…" Skye couldn't finish her question as the memories of her first dad came flooding back. What if she was sent away again? Was this all her fault? A small whine of fear escaped her lips. Old Dad reached down and gently patted her head. Tess looked at her sadly.

"Yes, Skye, it is the start of the scent of death."

"I didn't do anything! It's not my fault! Please don't send me away!" Skye blurted out her anxiety, a tremble in her body. Tess cocked her head and regarded her as Tag woke up and looked at them both, his nose slowly twitching from side to side.

"What's going on?" he asked.

"It's not your fault, Skye. No one will send you away; you're part of our pack." Tess got up and sat next to Old Dad, leaning against his leg.

"What's happ…?" Tag didn't finish his sentence as he too caught the scent. "Oh." He got up and lay across Old Dad's feet. The old man laughed at their antics.

"For goodness sake, dogs, you can't all be patted at once!" The children sent waves of love to Old Dad and hoped that he could feel how much they cared. Skye lay down as well, her small heart breaking once more.

Winter was long and cold that year and the three dogs spent as much time as possible shadowing Old Dad. This was harder than you would think, as Old Mum would not let them into their side of the house unless they were clean. This usually meant a good rub down with a towel to dry and clean the muck off their bellies and paws, and sometimes she even washed them with a cloth. They tolerated the fussing just so they could lie beside Old Dad and offer their love and support.

It didn't take long for Frankie and Benny to realise that the dogs were lying at the patio doors and that they couldn't chase them. So, cats being cats, they would deliberately stroll along the decking (even though they knew they were not allowed near or into the house), taunting Tag especially. The end result would be the three dogs having a barking fit at whatever cat was teasing them that day, wet noses smearing the glass and Old Mum sending them all out into the main kitchen, banned for the rest of the day. It took them a while to realise that the cats were doing this just to get them into trouble, which annoyed them even more.

Spring finally started to make itself known and Old Dad was getting worse. The babies could tell he was almost done. One day, all the humans piled into a car with Old Dad, their faces serious and anxious. The three dogs stood on the decking and watched as Old Dad looked at them through the window; as he smiled, they wagged their tails and said goodbye. He never came home.

The next few months were tough on all the humans; they were all very sad. Tag and Tess recognised the strange-smelling box when it arrived. It was the same as Aunty Jess, only this time it smelled of Old Dad. Everyone went into the woods again to the grove where Jess and Jook had been buried, and where a hole had been dug next to one of the trees. Skye cocked her head as she sniffed the ground next to the hole; she was sure she recognised something, something faint but familiar. It almost smelled like her first dad. Tess stepped between her and the tree, pushing her out of the way.

"Watch and learn," she said as the humans buried the box.

"Why are they doing that?" asked Skye, bemused.

"We don't know," Tag replied as he sniffed around Jook's grave, "I think they do it for comfort." Skye looked thoughtfully at the ground next to the new hole.

"I can smell my first dad," she said sadly, "Do you think they put him in the ground too?" Tess paused, standing on three legs, her front leg pulled up underneath her as she concentrated on what Skye had said.

"If they did, that would mean he was part of the pack." She snorted almost in disbelief. "That means you are also part of the pack." Skye blinked and took a deep breath.

"Does that mean we are related?" she said. Tag moved over to Tess and they both regarded the small dog in front of them.

"I don't remember you with my brothers and sisters," he said thoughtfully, "Maybe you are from another litter." He made a decision. "I suppose you are like a long-lost cousin." He winked at Tess, who tried not to laugh.

"I have a real family," said Skye as she trotted off as proud as punch back to the yard.

That summer, the whole pack went on holiday – Old Mum, Mum, Dad, Tess, Tag, and, of course, Skye. The whole of the back of the car was taken up by their beds so Dad was driving another car with all the luggage. They stopped to have a break and something to eat whilst the dogs got a chance to walk and relive themselves. It was very exciting! Skye was not used to being on a lead and kept pulling, which tightened the collar and made her choke.

"Stop pulling, idiot," snapped Tess, "You'll never break free so just follow what Mum says." Tess and Tag regarded Skye coolly as they walked obediently beside Dad, but Skye was a terrier and not good at taking advice. Mum, however, would not give in to the frantic wheezing coming from the end of the lead and a couple of good jerks made it clear to Skye that she better follow advice.

They arrived at the hotel and settled in their rooms, the babies sharing a bed and Skye on her own small basket. The rules were clear; the dogs could not be left alone in the rooms, so once breakfast was over, it was out for a walk before a drive to visit exciting places. The hotel was at the side of a sea loch and every morning, Mum would take the three of them down to the shoreline and walk along to a small peninsular where Tess and Tag could have loads of fun jumping in the water and swimming. Skye had never been a confident swimmer; she preferred to run up and down barking at the others having fun. Occasionally, Mum would catch her and throw her in, forcing her to swim and shutting up her yapping for a few minutes.

The road trips were the most fun. They would drive till they reached some woodland walks, then they would all run madly through the forest, taking in all the sights and sounds. Sometimes they would find a burn flowing deep enough in places for Tess and Tag to jump in and swim again. Tess especially had decided she really liked swimming. Skye would shout encouragement but stay safely on dry land. They learned how to behave when on the leads and in places where humans ate. Despite never being trained, they all lay obediently under the table, patiently waiting for their leaders to finish their meals. The holiday was tinged with sadness because Old Dad wasn't there. Old Mum did her best to stay cheerful, but the babies knew she was lonely.

When they returned home, it was almost as good as being on holiday. The children got to greet the other human members of their pack and boast about their adventures to the cats, who feigned disinterest but were intrigued. The rest of the summer fell into the usual rhythm and the weekly agility sessions started again. This time, however, Mum decided to let Skye have a go, but it was an epic fail. She couldn't see the point of jumping over poles she could run under, but she did like the tunnel, A-frame, and dog walk. When Mum tried to teach her the seesaw, everyone fell about laughing; because she was so small, the end hardly tipped down and it took ages before it was close enough to the ground for her to jump off. After a few weeks, Mum decided that agility just wasn't Skye's thing and she focused on Tag and Tess instead. Despite getting older, they were both lightning-fast, and even though they only managed one show a year, they still attained Grade Three level, though it didn't matter what level they were, just as long as they enjoyed it.

The end of another year was marked again as winter clasped its cold hands on the world, and there was deep snow again that year. The babies loved snow, but now Mum put their fleece jackets on to keep them warm as they ran about the yard. Skye especially struggled in the deep snow, being only a few inches off the ground at the best of times. It was a nightmare for her and she got cold very quickly, so Mum bought a fleece coat to match the others. Even so, she preferred to stay in as much as possible.

The snow that winter was deep enough for the humans to go sledging in the big field. The dogs absolutely loved this new game. They jumped about everyone excitedly as someone got onto the sledge (a large plastic board), then shoved off down the hill. Tag was in his element. Dad was great at this game, and a dog like Tag that loved to chase was fit to burst with the fun of it. As Dad hurtled down the slope, Tag was flat out following beside him, barking and snapping in fun at his head, daring him to go faster. Tess would bring up the rear, her sharp bark echoing across the snowy landscape. Skye would follow for a short distance but soon ran out of puff. One of the yard staff picked her up and held onto her as he sat on another sledge, then they were off! Skye's ears flapped madly in the wind as they hurtled down the hill. Tag and Tess followed, laughing and shouting encouragement, but Skye wasn't used to going so fast and quickly decided that sledging should be left to the humans. As soon as they stopped, she leapt away and ran back up the hill, struggling through the deep snow and out of breath by the time she reached the top.

"That was the fastest you have ever moved!" shouted Tag as he ran past her, his tongue hanging out of his mouth like a pound of gammon.

"I'm not built for speed, I'm built for digging," she replied as she burrowed a hole into the snow and flicked it high in the air. Tess shook her head as she bounded around the next human preparing to hurtle down the hill.

The patterns of life flowed as they had always done and the children were content. A truce had been drawn between the cats and dogs with each tolerating the other, an air of mutual respect between them. Spring brought the swallows back and this time they had a new story to tell, the story of the monster-catcher that defended their children in their nests. Tag would lie in the sun watching their aerobatics, wondering who they were singing about. Tess smiled to herself as she watched him. He was such a sweet and gentle boy, and she knew he didn't understand he was the hero of the story.

Sauntering over to him, she lay down and wriggled on her back, getting a good scratch. It seemed harder to roll about now as her body sometimes felt stiff. She lay on her back with her mouth open in a doggie grin as she watched Skye staring intently at a mole hill further down the yard. Intrigued, she got up and ambled towards her.

"Shhhh, be quiet," whispered Skye intently, "I can hear it." Tess paused and crept stealthily towards the mole hill. Skye was right; Tess could hear the scratching of the mole just under the surface. They both stared at the mound of earth as it began to move.

"Wait, wait," said Tess in a hushed voice as Skye tensed her muscles for the leap. "NOW!" There was a flurry of movement and Skye did a headstand into the loose soil, grabbing at the mole. She did it! She caught a mole! Tess barked in excitement as the small velvet animal was tossed into the air.

Neither of them knew what to do next as neither of them had ever killed anything. Tess pounced on it as it tried to run away, punching the small body firmly with her nose, just dodging the nipping teeth as the mole defended itself.

"Bite it!" shouted Frankie from her spot on top of the cabinets outside of the stables.

"What?" asked Skye.

"You have to bite it to kill it." Frankie sat up, her tail swishing and her eyes blazing as her predator instincts kicked in. Tess grabbed the small body but quickly spat it out as it tasted awful. Skye was undeterred and clamped her sharp teeth into the neck, tossing it high and killing it.

"Well done, smelly dogs, well done. You are almost as good as a cat." That was high praise indeed from Frankie. Tess and Skye wagged their tails, feeling very proud of themselves.

"What's that you've got?" asked Mum as she came across the grass. "A mole! Well done, you pair, you killed a mole. That is so difficult. I'm very proud of you!" They danced about her feet, shouting in excitement as she picked up the dead body and disposed of it into the bin.

"So you are now both mole catchers," said Tag with good humour, "Better go get the others before they dig up the entire yard."

Tess was hooked. This was a great game that didn't require speed but stealth, scent, and hearing. She and Skye had a competition going on, each trying to catch as many moles as possible. To be honest, Tess was very good at catching and Skye at killing, so they formed a team and the bond between them grew. This kept them occupied for most of the summer.

Tag was on patrol, trotting up the line of stables making sure everything was in order. He saw Benny sauntering towards him with a dead mouse in his mouth. He glared at Tag, the memory of the swallow incident still strong in his mind. Benny had never tried to catch another swallow, although sometimes he and Frankie would have a go at swiping them as they flew through the stable doors to attend to their young. He dropped the dead mouse, arching his back and hissing at Tag.

"It's dead, alright!" he snarled, "This is my breakfast!" Tag ignored him and continued down the stable block, pointedly passing right by him. Benny blinked slowly and flinched as the big dog paused next to him.

"What you eat for breakfast is your business, as long as it doesn't have feathers."

Benny grabbed his mouse and ran to the hayshed to eat in privacy. Tag continued his patrol around the stables, front and back, pausing to sniff the air blowing across the fields, then back round to the house to check if any new cars had arrived with clients who he would greet and welcome to the yard. In the past, he would have trotted the whole way, but now he just strolled at a leisurely pace. His body felt stiff sometimes and it took him a while to get going.

There was no holiday with the pack that year as

things just seemed too busy, so the children contented themselves with their agility and hacking with the horses (Skye, of course, simply would not go – she preferred to stay at home). Tag, as always, would thunder ahead on a hack while Tess was more sensible, staying just ahead of the horse. Mum had noticed that sometimes Tag just didn't seem to hear her calling him back. He would be a good distance ahead, running with joy and abandon, with Mum shouting his name to no avail. Tag was a very obedient dog, so it didn't take long for Mum to work out that his hearing was failing as he was getting older. She also noticed that neither of them was up to fast hacking anymore, running as fast as they could to keep up with the galloping horses, preferring the steady pace of the horse trot instead. Even though they were super fit, Mum knew they were both starting to feel their years.

It was yet another winter, this time long, wet and chilly. Tag and Tess had taken Skye's advice to stay indoors as much as possible and they felt better for it. One winter evening, they were in the indoor school for their agility session when Mum decided to let Skye have another go at it. The small dog had spent the last seven years jumping and running around the yard, so her body was as strong and muscular as the others. One of the other dog owners offered to try Skye as she was used to working with small dogs. Skye thought this was wonderful; she loved being the centre of attention, and having watched Tag and Tess over the years, she had a pretty good idea of what to do. The jumps were much lower to the ground this time (even Tag and Tess had been reduced to jumping smaller heights in respect of their age), so it was easy for Skye to work it out and she loved it.

At last, the three dogs could enjoy something together, and that winter was the best time for them all. The babies were now twelve years old and Skye eight, but none of them showed any signs of their age, keeping up nicely with the other dogs. It was the highlight of their week when training came around and they loved it.

The next summer was much better for everyone. It was a good mix of sun, warmth and showers, so the dogs didn't get too hot and could lie outside all day. That summer, Mum decided that Tess and Tag would have to retire from agility. She had noticed that when Tess was lying in her lap on the big seats upstairs, there was a strange whooshing sound in her chest as her heart beat. A trip to the vet revealed a heart murmur with tablets being prescribed. Tess hated her tablets and very soon learned that the treat of a cheese ball was hiding something nasty-tasting, so she began to spit it out. Old Mum had to trick her with a rolled-up ball of pate; it was so delicious that Tess swallowed it whole and never noticed the tablet. This became the new ritual for the children; every morning and evening, they would line up in a row and each get a ball of pate (even though Tess was the only one with a tablet).

That summer, Mum took Tag and Tess down to the field for a last go over the jumps. The field was on a small slope and despite her enthusiasm, Tess just couldn't do more than one round of fences. She finished the course and went and lay down in the shade, exhausted. Tag, of course, bounded out, but his hind legs were a bit stiff and even at the lower heights, he tipped a few poles – something he simply never used to do. That was the decider for Mum; no more agility and no more hacking. The babies were getting old.

The highlight of the year for everyone was another doggie holiday. A cottage had been booked and they all poured into the cars (Dad was in charge of the luggage while Mum and Old Mum had the children in back). Off they set on their road trip. Tag and Tess were old hands at this, lying dozing while Skye would sit looking out of the side windows watching what was going on. They stopped at their usual rest spots, feeling very privileged to sit with the pack leaders whilst they ate their lunch at a pub, passers-by patting them and making a fuss. Then it was back in the car and back on the road.

As the trip progressed, Tag began to feel more and more anxious. He was panting heavily, though not hot.

"What's wrong with you?" said Tess irritably.

"I… I… don't know," he replied, glancing around him, looking slightly confused.

"Settle down and stop being stupid!" Tess's worry

was hidden by her sharpness and Tag lowered his head submissively, his eyes darting around nervously.

Finally, they arrived at the cottage and it was simply the best place ever. The garden was secure so the babies were free to wander in and out of the house whenever they pleased. It was a home from home. Each day they would set out on a trip to find a nice woodland walk, just like the old days when they were younger. Their favourite was an old forest bordering a rushing river that cascaded down a gorge forming shallow pools that were deep enough to wade in and occasionally swim in. They all loved it, except for Skye, of course, who simply did not take to swimming at all.

Once everyone was tired out after such adventures, it was back to the cottage to rest up whilst the humans went out to eat. The children would lie happy and exhausted in their beds in the quiet cottage, Skye snoring, Tess upside-down and out for the count, and Tag lightly dozing, his eyebrows dancing up and down as he dreamed of woodlands and rivers.

All too soon, it was time to go home. They loaded up the cars once more and set off. Skye was restless; she was so nosy that she kept moving from one side of the car to the other. Tess tried her best to ignore her but was becoming irritable. Tag felt strange. His legs felt weak. He lay at the car boot door, his legs jammed against it, and struggled to sit up. He just could not get a purchase.

His legs wouldn't work properly and he began to panic and whimper. Mum looked in the rear-view mirror and saw him struggling.

"Tag's stuck!" she said in confusion. She pulled over as soon as she could and ran to the back of the car, opening the boot expecting to see Tag's tail jammed in it or something more drastic.

When the door opened, Tag regained his composure and sat up, wondering what had just happened. Mum was annoyed with him; he had frightened her and he was very sorry, but even he didn't understand what had happened.

"Tag! Stop being an idiot!" Mum snapped, shoving him away from the door. They set off again. A few miles down the road, Old Mum glanced round into the back to check on Tag.

"Where's Skye?" she asked. Morag felt her heart leap; surely they hadn't left her behind when they checked on Tag? She was positive she would have noticed her jump out.

"Good grief!" she said as she flashed Mark in the car in front, letting him know that she was going to have to pull over again. "Can you see her?" Morag asked Old Mum, who had twisted round in her seat to look.

"No!" Tess and Tag looked at each other; what a trip home this was proving to be! They knew where Skye was but they couldn't tell the humans. Mum got out again and opened the back door this time.

"Skye!" she exclaimed, trying not to laugh.

The large dog cushions extended further than the folded-down back seats, which stopped short of touching the front seats. This left a small gap leading into the footwell. This small gap was covered by the cushions; normally this was not a problem, as the dogs tended to stay well inside the back of the car. Skye, however, being nosey, was constantly wandering from one side to the other and had obviously stepped too close to the back of the driver's seat, standing on the edge of the cushion with nothing underneath it. She was now wedged upside-down in a headstand between the front and back seats. All that could be seen was her rear end and tail jammed in place by the cushion.

Mum had no idea how long she had been like this; it was funny but poor Skye was totally trapped, so, grabbing her back legs, Mum pulled her up and back into the car. "For goodness sake, you lot, get a grip!" Tess tried not to smirk at the small dog's discomfort as she gave herself a shake and felt the blood go back to her rear legs. Tag, however, was silent, a deep worry building inside him.

As the rest of that summer wore on, Mum noticed that at night Tag was struggling to walk if he had been lying on the hard floor at their feet in front of the TV. She asked the vets to check him while they were out visiting the horses one day. It was confirmed. Tag had arthritis in his hips. It wasn't bad at the moment but he was going to need something softer and more comfortable to lie on in the house. Two big soft dog beds were bought for the babies which lay in front of Mum and Dad's chairs, whilst several softer dog pads were dotted around the house in Tag's favourite spots. Mum called them the puppy cushions and they were great. Sometimes Tag could taste a strange taste in his food; it wasn't unpleasant, just odd. Mum said it was medicine to help his sore hips, so like a good boy, he ate it all up. Although the cushions were meant for Tag, sometimes Tess would lie on an edge, just to make a point that she liked them but didn't need them. Skye, however, knew she was not allowed, but sometimes at night when everyone was in bed and the door closed, she would creep to the big cushions in front of the TV and sleep on them.

That winter was hard on the babies in more ways than one. This was the first time ever they were not allowed to do agility. At night when it was a training evening, they would sit upstairs at the large patio windows and stare into the indoor school at the other dogs training. They just couldn't understand why they were not down there with everyone else. Mum and Dad felt terrible; the children obviously missed it so much, but they knew they were just too old. The cold weather was horrible on them too. Normally if it was cold, Dad would throw the ball for them to chase and warm them up, but now he was afraid he might hurt them so would only occasionally throw it a few feet away, just to let them know they could still play. All three dogs were happy enough inside the house throughout the day and didn't really miss hacking out.

First thing in the morning, Dad would let them all out to relieve themselves and Tag would do a quick patrol around the house, though sometimes he couldn't remember if he had done this and felt compelled to do one more circuit; it was all very strange. Tess watched her brother with mild annoyance as he absentmindedly gazed around the yard.

"What are you doing?" she said, trying to hide the niggle of worry inside of her.

"I... I... don't know, I think I have to check the boundaries for intruders, but I feel too cold."

"Intruders!" exclaimed Tess, "There are no intruders here, you've done your patrol. Come back to the house now." She trotted past him and he followed at a slow walk, a look of puzzlement on his face.

"What's wrong with Tag?" asked Skye as Tag pushed past her into the house.

"NOTHING!" snapped Tess. Skye put her ears down and dropped her head submissively, knowing better than to push matters.

It was a few days later that Skye really pushed Tess to her limit. She couldn't understand why she was so irritable; Tag's behaviour was getting strange and it worried her, so anything Skye did to annoy her would set her off into a rage. That morning, Skye pushed it too far. They were all trotting ahead of Mum and Dad – it was dark but not as cold today, so they were all going out to the yard for a while to help Mum and Dad work. In her excitement, Skye tried to push her way past Tess, who lost it completely. She flew at Skye in a fury, snarling and grabbing at the small dog's head. Skye ducked and snapped back, equally angry that Tess had attacked her. There was a flurry of teeth and jaws as both dogs tried to grab onto the other. Mum normally let them sort it out themselves and under usual circumstances, it would all be over in seconds. However, this morning, neither party would back down. They locked jaws and both shook their opponent mercilessly.

"TESS!" Mum's stern command would normally be instantly obeyed, but Tess continued to shake Skye.

"Let go!" yelled Tess to Skye, who was latched onto her mouth.

"I can't!" was the muffled reply as Skye frantically shook her head, trying to free her jaws.

"TESS, ENOUGH!" Mum was really angry now. With a crack, Skye flew to the side and they parted, Tess trotting away, licking her lips, her teeth sore. Skye tried to have the last say and made to have a go at Tess again. This was when Morag noticed the small dog's lip sticking out to one side.

"SKYE! COME HERE!" The ferocity of the command

was not to be questioned and Skye slunk on her belly over to Mum, who examined her mouth. One of the canine teeth on the top jaw was sticking out at a right angle, clearly badly damaged. That was why they couldn't part; their teeth had hooked onto each other and Skye, being smaller, had come off the worst. "Great! Another trip to the vet!" Mum knew she couldn't leave the tooth like that – it would have to be fixed or removed – so later that day, Skye was bundled into the car for a trip to the hospital.

When it was Skye's turn to be seen, they walked into the room with the vet eyeing Skye warily. Obviously, he had encountered Jack Russells before.

"Just put her on the table and tell me what's wrong." Morag noticed he didn't seem to want to touch Skye, so she picked her up and plonked her on the table, grabbing her muzzle and opening her mouth for the vet to see the damaged tooth.

"She picked a fight with one of the bigger dogs this morning and their teeth must have got locked. I thought you might be able to push it back into place."

The vet was feeling braver now he had seen how well-mannered Skye was (she knew better than to snap at people) and he gently examined the damage.

"Well, looks like she has fractured a piece of the upper jaw, so I don't think we will be able to save the tooth. It will have to come out."

"OK, do you want me to hold her?" Morag stared at

the vet, who looked slightly shocked.

"No, no, we will do it under aesthetic, it would be better that way." He quickly brought some forms over to be signed. "We can do her today if you want to come back later." Morag nodded and handed back the forms, giving the vet Skye's lead.

"Don't let her kid you on; we don't mollycoddle her. She is as tough as nails." The vet nodded and carefully led Skye away.

When Tess saw Mum arrive back at the yard without Skye, she actually became worried. Surely Mum had not got rid of her? She ran over to the car and sniffed out the story of Skye travelling; they had arrived at the vet, but she couldn't smell Skye returning, so she trotted into the house, glancing at Tag.

"What's the matter?" he said.

"Mum took Skye to the vet and didn't bring her back." Tess was circling the humans, trying to pick up what was being said.

"Has she given her away?" Tag stood and watched in bemusement as Tess cocked her head to one side.

"Wait a minute, let me listen." Tess sniffed the floor, pretending to be looking for crumbs. "Mum says she will get her later. Looks like she's coming home." She was surprised at how relieved she was to hear that. It was a bit of a love/hate relationship between them, and it wasn't till now that she realised she would miss Skye if she left.

"That's good. I wish you two would just get along." Tag breathed a sigh of relief and went to lie down under the table on one of his cushions. He needed to nap more often through the day and now seemed like the perfect time. Tess looked at him and shook her head, lying down next to him to wait for Skye's return.

It was evening when Mum came back with Skye and the babies ran out to greet her. Skye was a bit surprised that they seemed so pleased to see her and unsure if they really meant it.

"What happened?" asked Tess, sniffing her all over and scenting a strange chemical smell.

"I'm not sure. I sat in a cage beside other dogs," Skye began as they trotted back to the house, "Then someone picked me up and sat me on a table." Tag was fascinated. "I think I must have fallen asleep and when I woke up, I was back in the cage and my sore tooth was gone."

"Gone?" said Tag, sticking his nose under Skye's lip and sniffing at the spot where her tooth should have been. Sure enough, it was missing, the smell of blood strong.

"Get off!" exclaimed Skye, "It's still a bit sore."

"Sorry." Tag stepped back and Tess sniffed from a distance.

"I'm sorry too, Skye, for fighting." She lowered her head slightly. "Let's call a truce, no more fighting with each other." Skye looked at her carefully; she knew that with one canine tooth missing, she didn't have much of a chance in a fight with a big dog like Tess, so discretion being the better part of valour, she agreed.

"A truce – no more fighting." They both lay down, noses in paws, and went to sleep.

CHAPTER NINE

The sun gradually regained its strength, bathing the land with its warmth and encouraging the plants to wake from their slumber. Once more, spring was here. The longer days meant the dogs were out more enjoying the spring sunshine and breathing in the scents of new life awakening. As Tag lay one afternoon gazing out over the yard, a large raven landed on the fence next to him, studying him carefully, first with one eye and then with the other. The bird's feathers were slightly tatty and dull, its movements stiff. It clicked its beak and cawed.

"Well, well, fast doggie crow-catcher, it looks like we have both grown old." Tag looked up with his old dog eyes and squinted at the black bird. Realising he couldn't see him clearly, the raven hopped onto the ground near him and pretended to look for worms.

"Remember me, fast doggie? My tail feathers remember you." Tag looked again and slowly grinned as a faint memory came back to him.

"Surely it cannot be the same crow I nearly caught?" he exclaimed, "That was so very, very long ago." The raven cawed with laughter.

"I am a raven, actually, and yes, it was a long time ago. Twelve summer hatchings have come and gone since we last met. Many of my children have honoured our agreement and visited you, daring you to catch them too." The raven strolled closer and peered into Tag's face. "Your eyesight is failing fast, doggie."

"I'm not a fast doggie anymore," grinned Tag, "Those days are far behind me now." He extended his nose and sniffed at the black bird, a look of concern crossing his face. The bird laughed.

"I know, fast doggie, you don't need to tell me. For fifteen summers, I have danced with the wind and survived the harsh winters. My time here is at an end and I wanted to say farewell."

"Where are you going?" asked Tag. This bird seemed to be happy and unafraid.

"Somewhere wonderful, where the food is good, the wind is warm and strong, and there is nothing trying to eat you." The raven paused and sighed. "There is no reason to be afraid." He looked at Tag deeply. "You are afraid," he said. Tag swallowed hard and nodded.

"I am afraid sometimes because I feel lost. I forget where I am and what I'm doing, my mind is not here, then I am back. Do you know what that means?" He lowered his head between his paws and watched the old black bird preening a wing.

"I have heard that sometimes you don't go all at once to this wonderful place. You visit a bit at a time or leave a bit at a time till your body lets you go."

"Is that what death is? Leaving for a better place?" Tag was curious.

"That is what the roost legends tell, yes. For some of us, our time here is short. We want to move on faster. I liked my life so I stayed as long as I could, but now my body is worn and it is time to go."

"I don't want to go," said Tag, "For me, this is my wonderful place. I want to stay here forever." The raven stood beside him and made a strange chortle in its throat.

"Fast doggie, you will stay as long as you are able, but these bodies we use do not last forever. They must go back to the earth and feed the plants and animals that live there; that is the way of things. One day you will know that you must go and you will not be able to stop it. But do not have fear; there is nothing to be afraid of." The raven flapped his wings and clacked his beak, a loud raucous cawing croaking across the yard. "Farewell, fast doggie. Till we meet again, travel safe and stay happy."

"We will meet again?" said Tag in amazement, "In this wonderful place?"

"Of course we will. We are friends, remember?" The raven took to the air shakily and flapped away towards the woods. "Fast doggie nearly caught me, fast doggie crow-catcher." He sang his song till he was out of sight and Tag sat deep in thought.

The babies watched the cars being packed once more and knew they were going on holiday. Strangely, they were not as excited about it as the previous times. They would rather have stayed at the yard, but they would miss Mum, Dad and Old Mum if they went without them, so they reluctantly allowed themselves to be lifted into the back of the car to journey to the holiday home they had stayed at before. The familiarity of the place helped Tag be less confused, but they were both fourteen years old and looking for a slightly less active life, so pottering about the enclosed garden was enough for them. Tag, however, was restless. He wandered slowly in and out of the house even though his old bones ached. All the dogs were quiet. Tess lay at Mum's feet as she worked on the computer and Tag lay at Dad's feet when he became too sore to move.

"You alright?" asked Tess as she watched her brother lie down on the hard floor.

"Yes, just a bit tired. I have to keep reminding myself of the boundaries, you know, to do my patrol."

"You don't need to patrol here; this is not our territory. We are just visiting, remember." Tess licked her lips as she saw Tag looking a bit confused. Skye waddled over and sniffed at Tag.

"What's wrong? Why are you so worried?" She wagged her tail slowly in reassurance.

"Nothing's wrong, I'm fine. Leave me alone." Tag lowered his head and closed his eyes, drifting off into a light sleep.

One day, Mum and Dad lifted them into the car and took them to the forest trails. It was a place they had been to several times before and somewhere they loved to explore, climbing the steep path to the bridge and pausing only to swim in the river at the small breaks in the bank leading to the shallow pools. This time, however, there had been a lot of rain and the river was running high and fast, the waterfalls gushing with white foam as the water thundered down the hillside. Excitement at the promise of a woodland walk masked all stiffness and age in the babies and they bounded ahead, young dogs again, sniffing out the story scents of other people, dogs and wildlife that had left their trails along the way. They knew the path to take and ran ahead, Mum shouting them back when they got too close to the river's edge; she knew it was too strong a current for them now.

As the slope increased the pack slowed down, taking things at an easier pace till they reached the top and the wooden bridge. Tag stood proud and bold at the top, his eyes shining with joy, his tongue lolling out of the side of his mouth. Tess joined him.

"Well done, Tag, first again." She was a little out of breath as well, but they were still ahead of the humans.

Skye trotted past like a little battery-driven toy on automatic, and her low-slung body didn't seem to notice the slope at all. She sniffed the next path; they had taken this once before and it was a long way down in a loop back to the car park. Waiting patiently for Mum and Dad to catch up, they took in the beauty of it all, the scent colours making the picture far more vibrant than vision alone could do. Their humans finally arrived and stood on the bridge, watching the water from the impressive gorge thunder its way under them and down the hillside. A decision was made; they were going back the way they had come. No long loop today. They were off, back down the slope at a steady jog. It was easier for them to go downhill and they started to put a bit of distance between Mum and Dad.

"Follow me, I know where to go!" shouted Tag confidently.

"Slow down a bit, Mum and Dad can't see us!" Tess paused, unsure what to do as Tag's tail disappeared along the trail. "Tag!" she barked in annoyance, glancing back to see Mum and Dad just beginning to appear.

"I'll get him, you stay here." Skye thundered past like a mini rocket as Tess sniffed around waiting. Finally, Mum and Dad caught up with Tess and she trotted slowly ahead of them, scanning for Tag.

"Where's Tag?" asked Mum, anxiety in her voice. "Tag!" she shouted, but Tag's hearing wasn't good anymore and she realised he couldn't hear her. "Good grief!" They sped up as safely as they could. Skye came running back up the pathway towards them.

"Tag's in trouble!" she panted. Tess trotted faster,

following the terrier's tracks.

"Tess, come back here!" shouted Dad. Tess was frustrated. She didn't want to be disobedient, but she knew she needed to get to Tag quickly.

"Hurry up!" said Skye as she paused to peer over a small banking leading into the river. "He's stuck!" Tess ran barking and jumped down onto the stony shore, panic in her heart.

Tag was floundering in the cold fast-running water. He had scrabbled to the side but couldn't stand up, the cold seeping into his arthritic back legs making them numb and powerless. He was in total panic, flailing his front legs and trying not to roll under the water. Tess waded in beside him, unsure of what to do, while Skye stood on the bank, her tail a blur as she wagged it in anxiety. Mum and Dad appeared next to her on the banking.

"Tag, oh no!" Mum couldn't get down to the river's edge but Dad didn't hesitate. He jumped into the water, which for him was only just below his knees but was threatening to drown Tag. He grabbed Tag round the middle and lifted him up. The old dog was immobile with fear and his legs wouldn't support him. Lifting him higher, Dad plonked Tag back on the path where he lay on his belly shaking as Dad climbed back up, Tess shouting her encouragement. Slowly, Tag realised he was on dry ground and pushed himself up onto shaky legs.

"What were you doing, you stupid dog!" Mum was

trying not to cry and Dad rubbed his boy down, trying to stimulate blood flow. The heat from Dad's hands brought life back into him and Tag started to walk away, giving himself a good shake.

"Why did you go into the water, Tag?" Tess licked his face as she nosed him.

"I... I... just wanted to swim one last time," he said sadly.

"What do you mean 'one last time', you silly dog! There will be plenty of time for swimming." Tess shook herself and trotted off. "Come on, and stay away from the edge."

They continued back down to the car park, Mum and Dad deep in sad conversation, knowing that they could never bring the children back to this walk again. They were just too old. Tag didn't seem any worse for wear when they got home. He lay on his bed that night dreaming of rivers and pools with floating sticks to grab and chew.

The next day, they went on a different trip, this time to a beach they had been told about locally. Skye lay in the car watching Tag.

"I don't understand what your obsession is with water?" she said, never having taken to anything more than paddling.

"Just because your legs are too short to swim properly," sneered Tess, defending her brother's strange behaviour the previous day. Skye snorted and looked out of the window as the car drew to a halt.

Everyone bundled out and waited for their leads to be put on; Dad led Tess and Tag whilst Mum dealt with Skye. Off they went on a wooded pathway that finally opened out on a flat stretch of grassland leading to a sandy beach. It was perfect. Leads were unclipped and the three children ran off onto the sands, barking with excitement and looking for sticks to be thrown. It was the safest place to satisfy Tag's obsession with water and he had an absolute blast. Dad threw floating sticks just far enough for the dogs to wade out and drag back, Skye splashing in the shallows, barking her head off. Occasionally, Mum would pick her up and throw her in out of her depth so she had to swim back, which usually shut her up for a few minutes. One time when Mum picked her up, she paused just before she threw her and almost dropped her laughing. Skye wasn't stupid. She knew she would have to swim so she was already paddling in mid-air, winding herself up for the big splash. It was hysterical and Dad filmed it for posterity. That had been the best day for the babies; the sun was warm, the water was warm, and they had felt young again. It was hard for Mum and Dad too. Tag and Tess did not look like fourteen-year-old dogs; in fact, they looked fit and healthy and could be mistaken for eight-year-olds, but they knew that time was running out so they took as many videos and pictures as they could of this beautiful day.

Soon enough, it was time to go home. The dogs lay quiet and content in the back of the car on the long journey back, Tag's anxious panting the only sound from the boot. The rest of the summer was spent in the yard. Mum and Dad had decided on no more holidays with the dogs as the travelling was just too much for them now. So, as another winter finished and spring crept over the horizon, a holiday was booked without them, Old Mum volunteering to stay at the house to look after the children (to be honest, she felt she was getting too old to travel as well).

Tess sat staring at a molehill. She had perfected the art of hunting, sitting for hours patiently waiting for the mole to come close enough to the surface as it carried out excavations below and disposed of the soil. It was an easy game for her, involving little movement and the use of her nose. As she sat in the sun, half dozing and half listening, Benny strolled by. He was eight years old and in his prime, a real bruiser of a cat, muscular and lythe.

"What you doing, smelly dog?" he purred. Tess ignored him; she was a princess and it would be beneath her to snap. Benny sat and watched her, his tail coiled around his feet and twitching slowly back and forth. "Why do you hunt the ground mice? They taste bad."

"Actually, they are called moles and I hunt them

because they dig up the yard and cause problems."

"'Actually, actually' – my my, we are very polite, aren't we? For a smelly dog." Benny taunted her, daring her to chase him. He knew they weren't fast enough anymore. "I kill bigger prey," he continued, licking his velvet paw.

"Good for you. Why don't you get on with it then and leave me alone?" Tess lay down with her nose between her paws and Benny regarded her thoughtfully.

"I must say, it does impress me that you can catch these... moles. They are tricky." Tess opened one eye, suspicious that Benny was paying her a compliment. "Good luck with your hunt." He sauntered away, tail high and flicking from side to side. Tess raised her head and blinked; he had sounded like he meant it, but you could never tell with cats.

The dogs were in the house when it happened so they didn't see any of it. A horse had been brought in for training; he was an anxious traveller and visited once a week to work on his issues. Dad had been helping this horse for some time now and everything seemed to be going well. The horse was loading happily from the yard horsebox and into his own horsebox. On this day, the yard box was parked in the outdoor school whilst Dad loaded the horse in his own box in the car park. Benny had been hunting in the far fields that morning. With a full belly, he had wandered onto the yard to see what was going on. Benny knew to keep away from horses, so instead, he turned his attention to the yard box parked in the school, wandering over to explore the possibilities of a nice warm place to rest up and sleep. No one saw him going into the box.

Dad brought the horse around for one last session loading into the yard box in the school. The horse loaded then everything went chaotic; the horse was jumping and kicking in the box, the box was swaying from side to side, then in a flurry of movement, the horse ran out. Dad was holding onto the rope and shouting, "He's killed the cat, he's killed the cat!"

Everyone froze, trying to make sense of what was being said. Mum looked down and saw poor Benny lying at the side of the ramp, his body convulsing. As she picked him up, he lay still, blood trickling from one ear. "It's OK, Benny, it's OK," she said, knowing that it was not OK. Benny came to for a brief second and looked up at Mum as she cuddled him. He wondered what had happened, a small meow slipping between his lips, then he breathed out and everything went blank.

Benny had been in the box when the horse loaded, lying in the cargo store above the cab. Knowing that he shouldn't be near horses, he had made a fatal decision – a decision that had cost him his life. Jumping down to run out, he hadn't been fast enough. The poor horse got such a fright – he had only just begun to believe that horseboxes were safe when a predator had sprung down from above, triggering his flight instincts. The horse had lashed out and caught Benny squarely on the side of the head, knocking him out as he tumbled out of the box. It was a fatal kick. Curiosity really did kill the cat.

Mum laid Benny's body on top of the haylage bale as she knew Frankie needed to understand her brother was gone. The training horse had left and the dogs were let out, their noses telling them straight away what had happened. They sniffed around the spot where Benny had lain in the school, then followed the fading scent trail to the haylage bale, staring up at what they knew was Benny's body. Frankie had been hunting in the woods and came strolling onto the yard wondering what was going on. Her keen sense of smell told her something had died, but it was mixed with the scent of her brother. Tess and Tag looked at her sadly.

"Frankie, we are so sorry, but Benny is dead," they said as she slunk around the feed room and jumped on the feed bins.

From her vantage point, Frankie could see Benny lying on the bale as though he was asleep. She swished her tail slowly from side to side, her eyes blinking as she pondered on what had been said. Cats were not like dogs; they were not pack animals so the bonds of family were not as strong. But Frankie and Benny were littermates; they had grown up together and had shared this territory.

Together they had fended off invaders during the darkness of night – badgers, foxes, other feral cats. They had teamed up and fought to defend their territory. Frankie searched her strange cat feelings. Her partner was gone. As a predator, death was commonplace, but now it was the predator that was dead. She was sad – sad that she was now alone with only dogs for company, sad that she would have to defend the territory alone. She was getting older now, and younger cats had been coming around trying to steal their food.

She looked down at the dogs watching her with sad eyes. Pulling herself up with feline dignity, she jumped down from the feed bins and up onto the bales, sniffing and staring at Benny. "Farewell, fearless one, may your prey be slow, your claws be strong, and your teeth be sharp." She turned and jumped onto the rugs at the back of the shed, curled up and went to sleep. For a cat, that was that – she would mourn no more. Benny was buried in the woodlands with the others.

That summer, Mum and Dad went on holiday without them, but the dogs didn't mind; they were fussed and spoiled by Old Mum and their aunties and uncles. They spent their days trotting about the yard helping everyone. If they saw Frankie, they left her alone; a truce had been called and they would never chase her again. That winter was another cold one so most of the time was spent in the house lying with Old Mum watching doggie TV, letting yard life go by. Tag's face was almost white with age, his old eyes filmy and dull, making his vision poor. His hearing was going as well with sound seeming muffled, but his nose was still as strong as ever and it told him what was going on around him. Tess wasn't as stiff and sore as her brother. It was her heart more than anything that made her breathless, but the medicine in the pate kept her going strong. She was getting a bit more tottery on her feet, but she could see the decline in Tag. He really struggled to make it up the stairs to bed at night. Dad or Mum would support his back legs as he gamely pulled himself up. There was no doubt about it; they were old dogs now.

CHAPTER TEN

Another spring arrived and the babies were back in their element, lying on the grass in the sun. This was the best time for them. A strange worry sometimes plucked at them, a worry about leaving or missing Mum and Dad that would drive them to always be seeking their comfort, a lean on the leg or a familiar caress of the head, especially when Mum was in the office. They would take it in turns to wander in and stand beside her chair. "Always time for a puppy pat," she would say as she stopped what she was doing to gently ruffle their ears until they were satisfied and wandered off. As one left, another would arrive a few minutes later. Neither of them realised that it resulted in an almost constant stream of patting demands for Mum, who struggled to get any work done but did not want to miss the chance of showing her love for the babies.

Tag would often forget he had been in and would greet Mum as though he hadn't seen her all day. This confusion in Tag was worsening and it was getting on Tess's nerves. Sometimes he would blunder into her in a daze and she would snap at him in anger. Instead of retaliating, he would submit and apologise in a weak voice, which made Tess feel bad, and often if Mum or Dad heard her shout at him they would give her into trouble. Skye knew Tag was old and no longer top dog; now was her chance to move up the pack rankings, but somehow she just couldn't bring herself to do it. Tess was taking charge more, in a sad sort of way, so Skye just pretended she didn't notice and carried on as normal.

Summer was on the way and the family celebrated a very special birthday. Tag and Tess were now sixteen years old – a remarkable age for two big dogs. Tag's teeth were bad so they didn't get biscuits or toys; instead, they got human food! Cold meat in strips and pate, of course. It was great. One of the aunties had baked a cake and more than one piece of sponge with jam found its way to the floor to be gobbled up. But a few weeks after their birthday party, Tag had an episode. He was lying under the table at Mum and Dad's feet when he suddenly felt very strange. The world around him changed – he was lost, confused, dazed. Everything was spinning. He couldn't tell up from down and he panicked. He scrabbled with his paws, trying to get a grip on the floor, but it kept moving, his old back legs too weak to push him up.

"Taggy, Taggy, it's OK, Taggy." He could hear Dad's voice full of concern and he latched onto it, trying to bring everything back into focus. He felt Dad touch his shoulder gently and that allowed him to reorientate, coming to his senses and struggling off his side onto his belly. He lay quiet for a moment, a little dazed and unsure about what had just happened, Tess watching him, her heart breaking.

Mum and Dad decided then that the babies' beds would need to be moved downstairs; it was too much for Tag to go up the stairs now. At night, Tag would awake confused and pace up and down the bedroom, waking Mum and Dad. They wondered if he was looking for water so they decided he should stay downstairs where he could go into the kitchen for a drink. He seemed content to lie there in front of the fish tank on his favourite cushion. Tess was a bit confused when both beds were brought down, as she could go up the stairs fine, but realising what was happening, she resigned herself to the fact that she had to keep her brother company.

It was the hardest thing for Mum and Dad to go to bed each night without the babies lying next to them. Tag had wondered why they hadn't asked them upstairs, but in a way, he was relieved not to have to make the effort to get up the now very steep steps, so he turned and lay down on his soft bed and went to sleep, dreaming of ravens dancing in front of him, their tail feathers just out of reach of his teeth. Tess refused to lie on her bed; she found that the hard floor was cooler and more comfortable on her belly. She felt lumpy inside and it took her a long time to settle.

The new routine was established for the babies and, despite them being upset that they were separated from Mum and Dad at night, they were glad to be near their water bowl. Tess especially had a terrible thirst and would often get up for a drink during the night. The days were getting darker again and they could sense that winter was coming. In the mornings, they would all wander out onto the yard and go about their business, sniffing and relieving themselves. Tag didn't want to be out for any length of time, so as soon as he was done, he was back inside. He often tried to trot, but sometimes his back legs would give way as there was just no more power in them anymore. Skye watched Tag stumble and looked at Tess, who was pretending not to notice.

"Tess?" she said. Tess glanced at her and buried her nose into a strong smell in the grass. "Tess?" Skye persisted; she was getting old too. She was thirteen and her eyesight was foggy, but her nose and ears were as sharp as ever, her body a little more rotund than it used to be but still strong and active. Tess looked around at her, cocking her ear back to make sure Tag had got to his feet.

"What?"

"Can you smell it?" said Skye quietly.

"Smell what?" Tess knew what Skye was saying but didn't want to believe it.

"The smell."

"There are lots of smells, Skye, or maybe you didn't notice."

"The smell on Tag, faint but there," said Skye softly with sadness. Tess spun round.

"Don't you dare say it!" she shouted, "It's not true."

Skye stepped back and stared at her, her sharp nose telling her Tess wasn't angry; she was afraid. Deciding that she better keep her mouth shut, she trotted away into the house in a huff.

At night, Tess often lay half awake, keeping a watch on her brother. It was late autumn – the end of September – when it happened. Tess had nodded off, the gurgle of the pump in the fish tank and the murmur of the TV upstairs lulling her to sleep. She only half-noticed Tag get up and collapse against the door and filing cabinet. He panicked. Everything was wrong again. He couldn't get up and his legs wouldn't work properly. Flailing about, he banged on the cabinet with his feet, the noise alerting Tess, who sat up staring.

"Tag? Tag?" she said quietly as she watched her brother struggling. He lay still, panting, dazed and confused. Dad came running down the stairs and pushed the door open to see Tag lying on his side.

"Hey, old man," he said, gently patting his head, which instantly calmed Tag down. Dad was here; he was safe. Dad picked him up and put him on his bed and shouted for Mum. She came down, her face white with sorrow. Tag couldn't stand up. He knew Mum and Dad were upset and knew it was something he had done, but he couldn't remember what it was.

"It's OK, old man, it's OK." Mum and Dad sat beside him, stroking his head. Tess lay still, her nose telling her the truth. Finally, Tag fell asleep and everyone went back to bed.

The next morning, Mum and Dad got up early. Everyone was pretending to be cheerful, but inside, they were crying. Tag struggle to his feet determined to do his normal morning routine. Tess walked beside him.

"Tag," she said.

"I know," he replied, "I'm sorry, my pretty little Princess Tess, I am so tired, I just can't." His back legs collapsed and he lay down in the car park. Tess looked up in fear, Skye trying not to be noticeable in the background. Dad came running over.

"It's OK, old man, I've got you, my wee Tiggy McTaggle." He picked him up and carried him into the house, the others following behind. Mum dressed as Dad laid Tag down on his bed then went to get the car ready. Tess lay beside him, one paw on his bed, Skye watching from the back of the room.

"It's like a fuzziness, Tess, like I'm not really here anymore."

"Of course you're here. I can see you and smell you." Tess felt her heart ache; she knew what she really smelled.

"That raven was right, you know. I keep getting glimpses of the other place and sometimes... sometimes..." He tailed off and breathed heavily.

"Sometimes what, Tag?" asked Tess gently.

"Sometimes I smell Uncle Jook."

Mum and Dad came in and Dad lifted Tag up.

"It's not goodbye, my beautiful Tess. I will wait for you there." Tess watched as the door closed and she whined, lying down on Tag's cushion, Skye sitting beside her, not knowing what to say.

Tag lay in the car, tired and a bit confused. Part of him could see the other place, see Uncle Jook romping around and rolling on this back. The other part could see this grey world in the back of the car, a place that had fond memories of fun shows and adventures. The car stopped and the boot opened with Mum and Dad holding his head as he tried to sit up. Mum's hands – the best comfort he could have. When she held his head, all fear left him and he knew only love.

Two strangers came to the car; they smelled like vet and were softly patting him. Mum stepped back and Dad kissed his head.

"My good old boy, wee Tiggy McTaggle, Tagster the Dragster." He knew Dad was upset but he also felt his love wash over him.

"Don't be sad, Dad," he said, wishing his human could hear him, "I'm not afraid."

One of the strangers put a needle into his leg; he didn't even feel the sting. Mum held his head, her hands cupping his muzzle, her eyes looking into his. She leaned close to his ear so he would hear what she said.

"Where's my good boy? He's a good boy, Tiggy Tag,

such a good, good boy…" The words made him proud, made him happy. He was a good boy, his Mum and Dad loved him, and he wasn't tired anymore. The voice faded and an old familiar sound replaced it.

"There you are! I've been waiting!"

Skye heard the car return first and she stood up, alerting Tess. "They're back," she said. Tess joined her beside the door, her nose trying to pick out who was there. Mum, Dad, and… she felt her heart break. Tag. Dad came in carrying Tag on his bed and laid him down in his favourite spot in front of the fish tank. Tess and Skye looked at him. He was gone. He looked like he was sleeping, but they knew he wasn't there anymore; his name scent was fading and the death scent was strong. Dad went outside and Mum sat beside Tag. Tess came up and leaned on her leg, looking at her brother.

"I know, Tess, I know, he's gone, but he will come back and visit." Tess felt the sorrow and grief in her Mum; she wished that she could express her grief too. Lowering her head, she gently sniffed Tag's paws, taking in the last of his scent. She turned away; she knew what was coming next.

The door opened and Old Mum came in with all the aunties from the yard. Everyone looked at Tag and patted him as they said goodbyes. Then Dad lifted him up and carried him outside, with Skye and Tess following behind.

Tess expected them to go to the woods, but instead, they went into the back garden right next to the house. Dad had dug a hole there so Tag would stay close and not get lost. Everyone watched as Tag was laid to rest in the hole and covered, Skye and Tess sniffing at the edges before it was filled in, saying goodbye in their doggie way.

As they walked back into the house, Tess was despondent. What would she do without her brother? Skye tried to think of something to say; she had known Tag almost all her life and she was going to miss his gentle humour. Tess was old now too, and Skye's sharp nose would occasionally pick up that all too familiar scent. That night, Dad moved Tess's bed back into the bedroom and she strode up the stairs, her legs strong but her heart heavy with sorrow. She lay that night taking up the whole space that she had shared with her brother, his scent still strong on their beds. If she closed her eyes, she could imagine he was still there lying beside her.

The winter wore on and the special day midway through winter arrived, the day when the whole pack would gather with food and treats in abundance. This time there was no Old Dad, no Tag, and no favourite auntie. The pack was sad. Tess did her best to comfort and cheer everyone up, but she was struggling herself. Skye kept a low profile, knowing there was something very wrong and unsure how to make it better. Their days were spent lying together in front of the doggie TV, all animosity forgotten. One cold afternoon, they dozed side by side, basking in the warmth of the radiator next to them. Skye opened one eye then snapped to attention.

"Tess!" she whispered sharply. Tess wearily opened a bleary eye and looked at her.

"What is it now?"

"Look!" said Skye. Tess followed her eye line, her own fuzzy old eyes struggling to make out what she could see. There was a shape standing on the grass, a very familiar shape with a wagging tail. She opened her eyes fully alert and sat up; as she did so, the shape vanished.

"Did you see him?" asked Skye.

"Yes, yes I did." Her reply was almost inaudible.

"Has he come to visit?"

"Maybe. Maybe he is letting us know he is alright." Tess put her head back down, her instincts telling her something different.

When Mum came in that day to work in the office, Tess wandered through and stared at her. She turned around and smiled; Tess loved to make Mum smile.

"Hello, my pretty princess, want a wee cuddle?" Tess leaned on her leg and tried to tell her about Tag visiting, but she knew Mum couldn't hear her words. Instead, she accepted the kisses and patting before wandering off to let Mum get on with her work.

Tess was just two months shy of her seventeenth birthday. She had got up as usual, feeling a bit shaky but going through the normal morning ritual with Skye. As she turned to go into the house, she faltered; something was wrong and she felt very tired. Saying nothing to Skye, they went in and lay down in the living room. Today Tess decided to lie next to the fish tank. Their humans went out to do their morning's work and left the dogs to doze in the dark. Tess couldn't rest; she felt wrong. Skye lay under the table watching her.

"Tess, you smell…"

"I know," said Tess. She knew what was going to happen. "Listen to me, Skye. You will have to be top dog now. It's your job to take care of Mum and Dad." Skye whined.

"I don't want to be top dog. I want you to stay."

"I can't, I need to go."

"Go where?"

"I don't know, but I know Tag is waiting for me." She tried to stand and fell back down. "I can't walk, I am so very, very tired."

"Please don't go, Tess, don't leave me alone." Skye started to pant, anxiety building.

"You won't be alone; you have Mum and Dad."

"But, but, when I need to go, I won't know how to get there, no one will be left to show me." Skye was so upset that she began to walk in circles. Tess looked at her with weary eyes.

"Skye, I promise you won't be alone, I promise we

will wait for you."

"You will wait for me!" she said in disbelief.

"Of course, you are part of the pack."

Skye felt a mixture of joy and grief; she was part of the pack, but she had to watch Tess go. They heard footsteps as Mum and Dad came back in for breakfast. Skye ran to the living room door and Dad nearly fell over her.

"Skye! Get out of the way." He stumbled in and put the light on, immediately seeing Tess lying on the cushion and unable to get up. "Mo," he said, "We need to take Tess to the vet." Skye watched as Tess was lifted in her bed and taken to the car. She looked down on the small dog for the last time.

"I will wait for you. Take care of Mum and Dad." Skye couldn't answer. She simply sat on the decking and wished her friend farewell.

Tess lay in the car and remembered all the wonderful times she had experienced travelling this way to amazing adventures. She thought about her long loving life; she had a strong and powerful pack and had been protected all her days, which had been filled with joy and happiness every single minute. She was happy; she was content. The car stopped, the boot door opened, and she looked at Mum and Dad once more. She loved them so much and they loved her. Two people arrived and she lay back down, too tired to even hold her head up. Her leg was lifted and she felt a sharp stab. Her body was closing down and it was difficult for them to find a vein. She sat up and glared at them; she was a princess, they should get it right! Mum stepped forwards and cradled her head, Dad gently stroking her ears. She closed her eyes, her head resting in her mama's hands, the love in the touch reaching her very soul. Drifting away, she could hear her mama telling her what a good girl she was. Tess smiled to herself; of course she was a good girl. She was a princess, after all.

"Tess! Tess!" she opened her eyes as she heard Tag call her name. Then there he was in front of her, licking her face. "Tess, I've been waiting for you." He jumped around her excitedly, a young dog again.

She stood up. They were in a green meadow; the grass smelt fresh and full of wonder, and there was no pain in her joints, her strength and suppleness returned. She couldn't help but laugh at Tag.

"What are you doing, you silly dog!"

"Come on, come on." Tag ran ahead. She looked beyond him and saw old Jook, but he wasn't old anymore either.

"Where are we going?" she asked as she excitedly ran by Tag's side.

"Somewhere wonderful!" he said. Tess stopped and Tag turned round. "What is it?" he asked. Tess looked back over her shoulder. In the distance, she saw a grey cloud fading away.

"We need to wait for Skye, I promised."

"Yes, of course we will." He bowed a puppy play-bow. "Want to play chase?" Tess laughed and romped around with her gentle brother. They ran together, joy in their hearts as they knew that they had both been very, very good children.

Lightning Source UK Ltd.
Milton Keynes UK
UKHW040820090222
398402UK00002B/275